JOURNEY
BEYOND
2012

ALSO BY

PIERO RIVOLTA

NOVELS

The Castaway

Alex and the Color of the Wind

Sunset in Sarasota

POETRY

Going By Sea:
Poems & Thoughts for Today's World

Nothing Is Without Future

Just One Scent:
The Rest Is God

JOURNEY BEYOND

2012

PIERO RIVOLTA

FIC
RIVOLTA
06/12

NEW CHAPTER PUBLISHER

Sarasota 2012

Published by New Chapter Publisher

ISBN 978-0-9836184-0-9
Copyright © 2012 by Piero Rivolta

Library of Congress Cataloging-in-Publication Data

Rivolta, Piero.
  Journey beyond 2012 / Piero Rivolta.
    p. cm.
  ISBN 978-0-9836184-0-9 (hardcover)
  1. Prophecies--Fiction. I. Title.
  PS3618.I897J68 2012
  813'.6--dc23   2012005417

New Chapter Publisher
32 South Osprey Ave.
Suite 102
Sarasota, FL 34236
tel. 941-954-4690
www.newchapterpublisher.com

Journey Beyond 2012 is distributed by Midpoint Trade Books

Cover design and layout by Shaw Creative
www.shawcreativegroup.com

Printed in the United States of America

I dedicate this to everyone
who has spent time trying to restore
the primary qualities of life
that we all share as human beings:
intuition, compassion, common sense, love,
moral sentiment, admiration for nature,
appreciation for beauty and a sense of fairness;
and who understands
that just thinking and reasoning
in a strictly materialistic way
is causing us to live
in a constant state of fear and confusion.
Let the poet who is in all of us
share things in a simple, clear and direct way
so we can start a new journey
toward a renaissance in everyday life.

And to my wife Rachele,
who is living proof of the theory
that discussion and challenges in a marriage
bring about a long, healthy and positive life,
and will lead to love and forgiveness.

PART

I

❦ CHAPTER 1

Late one Saturday morning in October of 2011, George Hauser was looking out the window of his office at his engineering firm in Stamford, Connecticut. Because it was the weekend, he was all alone. The New England autumn was at its peak with maple trees everywhere glowing in red, orange and golden hues. The sailboats in the Long Island Sound were enjoying the breezes of the last weekend of warm weather before the descent into winter.

George reluctantly turned his thoughts back to his trip to Shanghai, where he was going to oversee the final stages of the construction of a large utility plant for the Chinese government.

He had come into the office to gather a few papers and to meet with his friend Ryan Morris, a finance manager and consultant who helped put together the deals that provided funding for Hauser & Sons' large-scale projects. Ryan had called George earlier that morning, sounding agitated and asking to get together right away. It was unusual for him to be so on edge, and George was concerned that there might be some unanticipated, last-minute difficulties. In fact, the call had unsettled him more than he liked to admit because the financial aspects were often worrisome. George was eager to finish up this project and get going on the next one, and he hated to be obstructed by delays and complications.

It didn't help that in the last few months, his wife, Valeria, had asked him several times to think about pulling back from his business, perhaps even leaving it behind for good, so they could spend more time together. There were moments when the idea appealed to him, especially when he had to deal with yet another self-important government functionary or bureaucrat who believed in applying idiotic rules and regulations to the letter, against all common sense. But for the most part, George loved his work and didn't feel the least ready to slow down. At 58, he was in his prime.

He glanced at the large black-and-white photo that hung on the wall behind his mahogany desk. In it, a broad-shouldered, middle-aged man was shaking hands with President Eisenhower. Both men were smiling, posing for the camera. George had been four years old at the time, and he vaguely remembered being there, lifted up by his mother so he could see his father and the president, although he had no idea at the time what it was all about.

George envied his father for working in what must have been a simpler, less demanding time when decisions were straightforward and uncomplicated, and projects could be completed without so much personal and bureaucratic red tape. He could not remember his parents ever arguing over how much time his father was away. But perhaps he hadn't witnessed it and, considering the turbulent history of his father's early years, was just casting a rosy-colored backward glance in time.

George's father, Hans Hauser, had been born in the mid-1920s in Germany into a solid middle-class family that had lived in the city of Hamburg for several generations. Hans' father, George's grandfather, was well-educated and enjoyed a fairly prestigious position as a builder involved in a wide variety of construction projects. His wife had originally come from England, but had spent most of her life in Lugano, Switzerland, where a branch of her family had moved.

But in the depth of the depression of Weimar Germany, the economy ground to a halt, and while the Hausers didn't exactly fall on hard times, lucrative jobs were not easy to come by.

So when the Nazis took over the government in 1933, George's grandfather was excited about the new, experimental projects, like the autobahn network, which was good and useful. But he soon grew disenchanted, especially when they started to prosecute and imprison political opponents of Hitler's regime.

By the mid-1930s, after grappling with his discontent over the deteriorating situation, George's grandfather made the difficult decision to leave Germany. Along with his wife and son, Hans, he immigrated to the United States. Because of his participation in several joint international construction projects, he had American friends who helped him to start over, but it wasn't easy. Although the whole family spoke English well, and had little difficulty adapting to their new surroundings, it took some time before George's grandfather was able to establish himself in his adopted country, succeed at the same professional activities he had pursued in Germany, and enjoy a certain amount of financial independence again.

For a while, he made trips back to Europe, but when the wrath of Hitler's dictatorship became unbearable, he lost all desire to continue his visits. Seeing his fatherland torn apart by the madness of the Nazi zealots humiliated him. By the time World War II broke out, America had become his home, and he dedicated all his efforts toward the Allied victory.

He instilled similar patriotism in his son. Hans served with distinction in the military, spending the war in the Pacific in the Army

Corps of Engineers. Upon his return, he took up the work begun by his father. It wasn't long before he was hired by a design firm that did business internationally, helping to reconstruct what had been destroyed during the war.

Hans had found his purpose in life. He enjoyed the many projects in the United States and Europe, and he did well, aided by the fact that he was fluent in English and German. By now his father was close to retirement and pulling back from the day-to-day concerns of the firm. As a result, Hans was so engrossed in working, designing and running the business, he didn't think much about the future.

It might have been difficult for such a busy man to find a companion with whom to enjoy a mutually satisfying relationship, but one day he met her in Germany. Mary Jane was an American who had first come overseas to work with relief agencies after the war and decided to stay on. She and Hans got married in 1951, and in 1953 George was born.

George remembered his mother as a warm, friendly, kind-hearted woman who had a good word for everyone she met. She created a comfortable home in Connecticut for both her husband and her young son, and kept up regular contact with Hans' parents. George looked forward to the Sunday afternoon visits to his grandparents' country estate. His grandmother would speak Italian with him and give him Swiss chocolate. His grandfather was more formal. He carried a cane and always wore a tie, even during their walks through the garden— which struck George as a bit odd—but he enjoyed listening to the stories the white-haired man told about the construction projects he had led and how he dealt with the inevitable challenges along the way.

With his head full of exciting tales about building from an early age on, it came as no surprise to anyone that George carried on the family tradition and became an engineer. After he finished his university studies, he interned at a number of other engineering companies, working on a variety of big projects in different countries, before join-ing his father's firm.

He discovered that, unlike Hans, who was more of an inventor, his talents lay in organizing and dealing with different cultural situ-ations. Aided by a knack for acquiring languages—he was fluent in German and English, and could get by in French and Italian—he had the ability to streamline and simplify complex problems and to explain them to the representatives of the governments and big corporations that employed him in a way that made them comfortable and engen-dered trust. He actually enjoyed what other engineers experienced as a necessary evil—dealing with people. George credited his grandparents for passing on to him gregariousness and the ability to get along with a wide variety of different personalities.

George and his father made a great team and the firm prospered. Then, in 2001, Hans died quite suddenly from cancer. The bereft Mary Jane, who had been suffering from heart disease herself, was so distraught that she succumbed soon after. George was beside himself with grief. If he had not been married to Valeria by then, he would not have known how to cope. With her deep empathy and intuition, she realized that his mother had lost all reason for living, and she told George that it was because of her great love for Hans. It was small comfort, but helped a little.

As it was, the loss of his parents devastated him. They had been an anchor in his somewhat chaotic life. But with Valeria's support, he refused to give in to despair and soon threw himself into his work, keeping busy and racing from project to project at a furious pace. As a result, the firm reached levels of success his father never would have imagined.

Still, George missed being able to consult with him, if only to hear his voice, which always had provided support and encouragement. Now he was poised to really make inroads into the Chinese market.

This project was bigger than any he had done there previously and if it succeeded, he knew others would follow.

A knock at the door roused him from his reverie. He went to answer it, and there was Ryan looking disheveled, carrying a briefcase and his winter coat. He wore only pants, a shirt and a sweater, and his hair was uncombed. His dark eyes, which usually darted about with lively curiosity, were red-rimmed and shone with the burning intensity of a man who hasn't slept well in days.

Ryan must have noticed George's look of concern because he said right away, "Don't worry. It's not what you think."

George was taken aback, "So this is not about China or any other project we have—"

"No, no…nothing like that," Ryan interjected. "Everything is going well. I need to talk to you about something else, something big, something important—very important!"

George felt relieved, but remained uneasy. He had never seen his business colleague so agitated and unkempt. Ryan was usually a meticulous dresser. His suits were expensive and elegant. Even on the golf course, his outfits reflected the latest fashion, so seeing him in a wrinkled shirt and pants that he seemingly had slept in was disconcerting.

To recover his bearings, George invited Ryan into the conference room adjacent to his office. Ryan opened the briefcase, withdrew a book, and with a flourish placed it on the table and pushed it across to George. He may have been rumpled and scruffy, but he had not lost his flair for the dramatic.

The title on the cover was written in Italian: *2012—la fine del mondo?* George recognized the author, Roberto Giacobbo, a well-known personality on Italian television.

He looked up at Ryan, who was watching him with eager anticipation. "2012—The End of the World? You can't be serious."

Ryan burst out, "I am! I have been reading everything I can get my hands on about the Mayan prediction of the cataclysmic events that will happen on December 21, 2012. I just came across this book, but since I don't understand Italian, I need you and Valeria to read it and explain it to me—so I can compare it to the other books I've read."

George was incredulous. For a moment it occurred to him that Ryan may have cracked under the pressure of work and gone mad. He looked too serious and intense to be playing a practical joke.

Ryan seemed to anticipate his concerns once again, "I'm not crazy. If any of these predictions come true, we have to prepare ourselves for whatever is going to happen next. Of course, it's also an opportunity to make a lot of money, but unless we know what's ahead, we can't proceed in the right way. So do me this favor. It means a lot to me."

Hearing Ryan talk about making money reassured George somewhat. This was the Ryan he knew, the man who sniffed out profitable deals in the most unlikely situations, who always came out ahead during market fluctuations, who had foreseen the recent worldwide recession and real estate crash in the United States and had used the opportunity to amass considerable wealth for himself.

Still, this was different, leading George to ask, "But what got you interested in this?"

Ryan seemed to relax for the first time since his arrival. "A woman I dated told me about it. At first, I thought she was just one of those 'new age' crackpots, but she was very attractive, so I decided to go along with it. Then I got interested and realized there might really be something to it."

George smiled. It sounded credible, given Ryan's reputation as a bachelor and womanizer, but he wasn't sure if that was all. At times like this, George wished he could read Ryan's mind.

He decided to play along. So much of the success of his business depended on this man's talent for successfully negotiating the waters of international finance; humoring him in this foolishness was the least he could do.

"Okay," he said, picking up the book and giving it another cursory glance. "I'll take it with me on the flight to Lugano and have Valeria read it as well. We can talk about it when we meet up in China."

Ryan looked relieved and pleased. "Thank you. You know how much I value your and Valeria's opinions."

George nodded, although he didn't really believe him. He was well aware of Ryan's independence and cunning in dealing with others. In George's experience, he was nothing if not devious, and not only in his relentless pursuit of financial success. He just hoped that this was a passing fancy and wouldn't turn into an obsession that limited Ryan's abilities and effectiveness as a business partner.

CHAPTER 2

The flight from New York to Milan was calm and uneventful. George appreciated the smooth trip because the situation with Ryan continued to nag at him. As he leafed through the book, he wondered once again how a man so versed in the ins and outs of international finance had allowed himself to become obsessed by what George considered, at best, an interesting mental exercise.

Unless Ryan was just looking for another angle to make money. He was something of a financial wizard, of that there was no doubt. His business continually prospered, especially in times of crisis, as other enterprises were devalued and could be bought up for next to nothing. The fact that it spelled ruin for people who had worked many years and dedicated all their energy in a given sector did not concern him. He often would juggle the budgets of failing companies, find fresh capital, issue stocks and then launch them into the world like new toys with an uncertain future. If, in the process, he destroyed companies that employed people who created ideas and products that contributed to the evolution of the world, he didn't care. What thrilled him was the gratification of a financial operation that played out simply and yielded positive results for his hedge fund clients.

What thrilled him even more were the commissions and earnings that flowed into his bank accounts. Making money and watching his fortune grow were the only things that really mattered to Ryan.

Not that he eschewed the trappings of success and the prestige that came with them. He had a beautiful office in Manhattan—not large, but quite elegant and stylish, with a small yet efficient and professional staff. In short, he'd created the perfect surroundings for himself on Wall Street, center of all those magical global manipulations at which he excelled. He'd opened branch offices in Shanghai and Singapore, and worked closely with other outfits in the UK, Switzerland, India and Dubai.

Nor did he skimp on the social benefits his wealth conferred upon him. He wore expensive, elegant clothes, frequented the most exclusive restaurants, and hooked up with the type of women that frequently landed him in the society pages. But all of that was secondary to his real purpose in life—chasing after wealth and amassing a big pile of money.

George had long understood Ryan's character and way of doing business, and although he appreciated the result, he did not always like his methods. It bothered him that Ryan procured the funds for their various projects using potentially shady means and hurting hardworking people along the way. Sometimes Ryan actually would bet against projects that were being carried out with great skill when he knew they might come to a halt due to lack of sufficient funding and the nightmare generated by the banks. In these cases, his participation sometimes led the project to the brink of failure, and the people involved would risk losing everything in the wake of his financial and political manipulations.

George remembered one day discussing such a situation with Ryan, who said, "What does it matter? They weren't able to go on with the project. In war it's the victors that survive. The others die."

"That's just the thing that puts me on edge," George said. "First of all, in war even some of the winners perish. Oh, I know they're the ones who don't count very much in the victors' estimation, but they do die, and what for? All that massive destruction doesn't really change things fundamentally. It just lines the pockets of the few."

"Well, don't you want to be among those few?" Ryan interrupted. "What matters is that humanity works to create food, jobs and amusement for people, and earnings for me. But war encourages the creation of lots of new things. It accelerates the world's creativity."

"Agreed," George admitted. "But that doesn't mean that those kinds of products are really necessary. Then again, if they do get invented over a longer period of time, what's wrong with that? We've been on this Earth for thousands and thousands of years. What difference does one century more or less make? In any case, I find the exploitation propagated by the world of high finance distasteful and unsettling."

"Well, I don't," Ryan said. "And how is that different from earning a good living by making sure that construction companies don't waste time and money? Money's always part of the equation."

In that regard George agreed with him. Wealth was not necessarily a negative thing—on the contrary, it could be positive when used to help the world become more coherent by pursuing humanity's basic needs and simplifying life. What George hated was that all too often it was used to feed power and complicate everything. Men like Ryan could dispense with creativity, knowhow and intelligence linked to future improvements, because all they need to do is make a science of hypocrisy—the way they perfected it on Wall Street over the past few decades, while bringing the world of real work and productivity to its knees.

George knew there was really no sense in arguing with Ryan about this, so he let it go. When work was finished that day, each man went his own way, convinced of the truth of his own respective ideas.

Looking out the window of the plane, George took a sip of scotch. He considered that now Ryan seemed to have found something new to fixate on, and George had no idea why. He found himself missing Valeria. She had a soothing presence and a unique approach to problems, a combination of intuition, meticulous research and thoughtful analysis, which always gave him a new perspective on things. George was eager to reunite with her and he was curious what she would make of Ryan's odd obsession.

In some ways, she knew Ryan better than he, although George had worked with him on numerous projects for more than two decades. She and Ryan had had a brief relationship before George met her—in fact, it was Ryan who had introduced them.

❧ CHAPTER 3

It was in early summer of 1995, on June 23 to be precise. George remembered the date because they got married exactly one year after they met, almost to the day.

After spending a year and a half in the Middle East, with only a few brief trips to the United States and Europe for technical and organizational meetings, he'd grown weary of being abroad. He enjoyed his work and watching his projects thrive, but life in Dubai and the United Arab Emirates was somewhat strange and terribly boring for George. All that exaggerated luxury seemed false and forced, and relationships with both the local inhabitants and resident foreigners proved extremely superficial. Amusements lacked any kind of soul, and there was not that profound sense of culture and tradition which, even though worn thin and often ignored, bonded Europe and America.

The desire on the part of up-and-coming nations to emulate and appropriate the sensational and decadent aspects of the Western world filled him with a sense of pity. Only the most expensive cars, the biggest boats, the fanciest buildings and the hottest designer brands seemed to matter—as if people couldn't choose things simply because they liked them. Of course, the paradox of paying more for something with a famous label on it, even if another product was more pleasing, had originated in the West. Even polo shirts had to bear a logo, a name or an animal to be considered worthy of wearing them.

George often mumbled to himself, "If someone wants me to put on his brand and promote his product, he should pay me."

This nonsense was by now deeply ingrained in societies throughout the world, but in the Middle East it appeared to have attained preposterous dimensions, as a consequence of new wealth obtained from nothing but the oil in the ground, not by means of hard work or ingenious ideas. This change had come about too quickly. The old traditions, although not erased altogether, were relegated to the background. The new world had mesmerized people's imaginations with the promise of a life that was easy, peaceful and safe. No one ever wondered whether or not it were all true.

George felt in need of at least a month's vacation. His contribution to his most recent undertaking was coming to a conclusion, and he had several new projects already lined up, but for the first time in his career he was not looking forward to them. He had been going at it full tilt, expanding his father's firm by joining forces with a small but efficient group of collaborators in the United States and Europe. He'd opened a branch office in Switzerland where he could work with colleagues from Germany, France, Italy and the Netherlands, all countries that were very active on international markets. But now the heady excitement had run its course and he was beginning to feel burned out.

One evening in Dubai, George was invited to dinner by an American he had met on several business occasions while working on projects in the Middle East. That American, Ryan Morris, was about 10 years George's junior, a young man on the make, always brimming with ideas about how to generate more money. George had enjoyed his lively company the times they'd gone out together before.

That evening Ryan was playing host to a man and two young women from Europe who worked for a large company that organized vacations and cruises. Did George want to come along? On the spur of the moment, he had said yes.

As usual, Ryan was the center of the conversation, which was fine with George. It allowed him to hang back, relax and enjoy the company without having to exert himself and perform. The two women, Giselle and Valeria, were lively and good-natured. They worked in the Lugano office of an international travel firm, while the man, who was a bit boring and whose name George soon forgot, worked in the Genoese branch. Giselle, dark-haired and seductive, knew how to put forth her best features and possessed a wicked sense of humor. Valeria, whose long, blonde hair enveloped her face, was not beautiful in an attention-grabbing way, but a combination of quiet attractiveness, elegant gesturing and the sparkle in her eyes made her strangely appealing.

She and Ryan seemed to be on familiar terms. From the easy way they laughed together and touched each other occasionally, although there was nothing flirtatious or sexual about it, George surmised that they had known each other for some time and perhaps had had an affair at one point or another.

Away from their respective environments, they all felt they could let the conversation drift wherever they wanted and voice their opinions freely. It seemed like the fresh sea air from the Persian Gulf had invaded the restaurant. Among good food, wine and much laughter, they discussed the various vices and virtues, the positive and the negative aspects of the different places they'd visited and the people they met along the way. There were plenty of interesting anecdotes to share.

Later, when they headed to another nightspot, George was surprised to find that he was having such a good time, he would be happy for it to go on all evening long. Usually, by this point in a night out on the town, he was ready to return to his apartment, either alone or with a woman who was not looking for a serious long-term commitment. He had had a few relationships and friendships with women here, but none of them had any potential for a real future.

That evening George was truly enjoying himself. Perhaps the two women reminded him of the way his grandmother talked, and he peppered his speech with the little Italian that he remembered, and was pleasantly surprised when the others understood him.

At a certain point he took advantage of his companions' professional travel credentials and told them how he was desperately in need of a month's vacation. "I want to find a place where life is simple, pleasurable, with a bit of activity, and where good eating, drinking and sex are considered straightforward, happy components of life that do not need to be the source of complications, conflict and dramatic scenes."

Valeria, who had encouraged George's attempts to speak Italian, smiled and said, "George, you've just described Italy! It's a country that's tough to work in because of its absurd political system, and there's a crazy amount of bureaucracy. But the Italians, after the fall of Rome, over centuries became accustomed to living under various regimes, as well as under the rules laid down by ecclesiastical governance. That has taught them one important thing: to focus on making the best of life and not giving a hoot about all the rules. They always come up with a solution to any problem. When you observe them more closely, you notice that many of them feel like citizens of the world. You can find them everywhere, working, living, investing capital. But even if they criticize their own country, they always feel great nostalgia for it."

"The secret is to go to Italy on vacation, spend some money, but not get involved in their problems. If you take it like that, visiting Italy is really very pleasant. If you like, I can whip up a basic itinerary for you, that is, if you're interested."

It was the most she had uttered all evening, and George couldn't help but be impressed by the combination of historical analysis and good common sense. Although he'd been to Italy on business, he'd never looked at the country from this perspective.

"I'm very interested," he answered readily, "but I wouldn't want you to waste your time. My work life is so complicated, sometimes I have to change my plans on short notice and end up not being able to go through with previous arrangements."

Valeria continued, unfazed, "Don't worry, for me planning trips is fun, even if they don't work out. It's like revisiting my favorite places. I'd need to find out a little more about your tastes, though, and what kind of traveler you are, to make sure I come up with the perfect plan."

For an instant, George sat in silence, trying to figure out how to answer her. Was she expressing more than a passing interest? It dawned on him that he would have to discuss this whole thing with her in detail, and that he was actually looking forward to it.

"How long are you staying in Dubai?" he asked. "We would have to meet and talk about it another time."

"I'm in no hurry to leave. My plans are still a little vague. I'd be happy to get together again to discuss your vacation, if you want to."

George was pleased by her answer, and so they agreed to meet up the next day.

Even now on the plane, George still remembered Valeria's face as it appeared to him that night, and the following afternoon when they met to look into various options for his trip. He was fascinated by her approach, a combination of poetic, practical and philosophical considerations. In those days he had his first taste of how everyday life, work and close relations could become quite interesting when you dealt with others from different backgrounds and traditions.

He learned that she was well-educated with degrees in literature and history. She was enjoying her travels all over the world to check out locations for her agency, but didn't think she wanted it to become her career. At some point she confessed that she pursued astrology as a hobby, and looked at him in a teasing, yet challenging manner, as if to dare him to argue with her about it. George surprised her by expressing more of an interest than she would have expected from a rational engineer.

Valeria also confirmed George's hunch that she and Ryan had had a brief relationship. They had met in their early 20s in New York when she was studying Egyptian history there. George didn't care one way or another. What mattered to him was that Valeria opened up new ways of understanding and seeing for him.

It didn't all happen during this brief stay in Dubai, but grew with each new itinerary she planned for him. On one occasion she said, "Why don't I come with you?" and so they started to travel together. There was no formal decision or acknowledgment made, it just kept happening more and more often, and they discovered that they were a good fit.

George met her several times in Lugano while staying at his family's house, and their relationship grew quickly.

At some point, Valeria introduced him to her parents. Her father, Carlo, was a retired Italian diplomat and had served his country as an attaché and ambassador in different parts of the world, including South America, Europe, the United States and the Middle East.

His wife, Sylvia, came from an Italian aristocratic family and was open to new ideas and lifestyles. Elegant and charming, she was an amiable hostess who made George feel at ease with no apparent effort. He could see that Valeria was her mother's daughter both in appearance and temperament.

After dinner Carlo took George into his study. Over cigars and brandy, he asked him about his future plans with the subtle interrogation techniques of a seasoned diplomat. Apparently George passed muster, because Carlo instantly became less formal and told George that when he and Sylvia had gotten tired of crossing oceans and changing homes and languages, they had retired to Lugano, close to the country they had served all their lives, but removed from its daily problems.

Back in Connecticut, when George told his parents about his engagement to Valeria, his mother burst into tears and threw her arms around him.

His father was moved and embraced him as well, saying, "I thought you were immune to getting married. In fact, I had lost all hope that you ever would consider it! But I couldn't say anything to you because I got married rather late in life, practically at your age, just like my father. I was against it for some time, but I can tell you, once people like us finally decide to get married, their ties are as strong as reinforced concrete."

When George's mother rolled her eyes, he chuckled and gave George a playful slap on the back. "Between us engineers, we understand."

They got married in Connecticut in a small, intimate ceremony. Valeria's parents flew in from Italy. For her father, it was his first time back in the United States since he had retired from the diplomatic corps. Ryan came up from New York to attend the wedding. He and George had continued their friendship as George had learned to appreciate Ryan's financial savvy and involved him in some of his latest projects.

Ryan proved to be an invaluable asset over the years, smoothing out the concerns of large clients by helping them figure out how to best finance their construction projects. George had to admit that he had come to rely on Ryan's advice a good deal; it was always sound and grounded in reality.

And now he seemed to have given in to some strange flights of fancy.

🔆 CHAPTER 4

Halfway across the Atlantic ocean, George once again picked up the book that Ryan had thrust at him with such agitation and started to read. It was easy to comprehend, written for the general public, with a dash of sensationalism to be expected from a television figure used to dispensing hype and melodrama.

The book provided clear historical, religious and astronomical references that indicated December 21, 2012 would be a turning point of great change for planet Earth, especially for the lives of *homo sapiens,* the only species with consciousness and the ability to have posed the problem. Other species either ignored the issue or did not perceive it at all. In any case, they simply exist or act the way they do because it is their destiny.

George recalled a discussion he had had with Valeria about cataclysmic events. Drawing on her background in history, she had argued that whenever sudden changes occur, they tend to spark predictions of the end of the world, which, of course, hadn't yet materialized. The notion of the apocalypse was deeply embedded in the human psyche, and in mythology and religious lore, from the Norse *Götterdämmerung* to the Book of Revelations in the New Testament.

George agreed with her. While this planet had certainly seen its share of enormous catastrophes in which entire species were wiped out, life has continued regardless of what people have to say about it. *Homo sapiens* likes to talk, theorize, take on ideas and argue about such events. And then what? He goes to sleep exhausted yet satisfied with the time spent chattering about the fate of the world, as if everything depended on the actions and will of human beings alone.

As for December 21, 2012, George mused that it might even be a stroke of luck for mankind if on that day the Earth were to be hit by a meteorite that wiped out two-thirds of the world's population. At least the remaining third would be left to rebuild. If the survivors learned any lessons with regard to past mistakes, which George doubted, they might create a whole new set of laws to live by, including one which would prevent overpopulation from occurring again.

George didn't care whether or not he was among the two-thirds of the world's population that was doomed. For him, it would be no different than dying in a plane or car crash. As someone who traveled a lot, he accepted the risk and if it happened to him, so be it.

George met Valeria at Malpensa airport in Milan as he emerged from the gate with his carry-on bag. There she was, waving, beaming, her soft features framed by her short blonde hair worn pageboy-style. George had a fleeting image of how she looked with long hair when he first met her, but that was many years ago, when youth meant showing the world all you've got. The woman of the 21st century that stood before him appeared to be in perfect step with the times.

They embraced and walked toward the exit arm in arm.

As they drove north toward Lugano, George could make out the Alps in the distance and felt himself relax for the first time in weeks. They didn't say much after their initial greetings, just a few routine comments, the way people who haven't seen one another for a while are wont to do.

For much of the drive, they were content to exist in the silence of each other's company. Like many seasoned couples, they didn't need to fill the air with idle chitchat to feel connected, but picked their moments for deeper conversations. Thus, they did not discuss Ryan during the hour-long drive, although George had mentioned his obsession with 2012 to Valeria when they had talked by phone before he left Connecticut.

Valeria was a fast and sure driver, and before long they passed the city of Como and crossed the border into Switzerland. The weather was clear, and the green mountains surrounding them, much lower than the Alps farther to the north, were a pleasant change from the urban sprawl of the tri-state New York area.

George was not only looking forward to spending time with Valeria, he also loved Lugano, his home away from home. Thoroughly Swiss in character, Lugano was also a cosmopolitan town, beautiful and relaxing, favored by high-powered, wealthy retirees from different countries who had worked out favorable financial terms with the Swiss government. As a result, George and Valeria had met a number of interesting people and developed a small circle of friends whose company they enjoyed.

Like George, Valeria loved Lugano and its lake, but she also liked being so close to Italy. There life was always a bit chaotic, especially in Milan, a city whose variety, culture and excitement were immensely appealing to her. If she felt too isolated at home, she could always visit the city; and if things got too hectic for her in Milan, she could withdraw to her quiet Swiss town. She often mused that only Italians could be truly comfortable with their tumultuous existence and enjoy the often bewildering hubbub that characterized their daily lives. Still, anyone who recognized the reason for Italy's vitality at all couldn't help but fall in love with the country and try to spend at least some time there at regular intervals.

For Valeria, who gave up her career when she married George, living like a well-to-do, occasional commuter was a blessing. George had wanted her to be free from the mundane, day-to-day requirements of a job, so that she could better pursue her passions—history, psychology, the spiritual aspects of religion, and astrology—and travel with him when his work took him to far-off places for months at a time. He was earning plenty to support them both, and Valeria had some money from her family, so they were able to live comfortably.

She thought about George's request for some time before agreeing, but once she made up her mind, she had no regrets about leaving her career behind. Since then, they had been happy to live, if not extravagantly, then contentedly, never lacking for the means to do what they wanted.

The two of them were well suited to one another. As in the early days of their relationship, they enjoyed traveling together and getting to know new and different kinds of people. If curiosity is one sign of intelligence, they exemplified it, living to explore the world and all the wonderful things in it.

There really was something beyond their daily lives together that bonded them. Both were well-read, especially Valeria, and after immersing themselves in the thoughts of philosophers, theologians, believers and non-believers, they'd reached a conclusion: You have to live and live intensely. Perhaps one day, in an instant of space and time, or in something that is neither space nor time, we will find the answer to the question of our existence that has been lurking in our minds since the dawn of time.

The most difficult challenge they encountered was the fact that they did not have children. They had tried for some time, although they never resorted to the measures and treatments some couples pursued at fertility clinics. As Valeria grew older, past the age of childbearing, they talked a little about adopting, but in the end decided against it.

Valeria faced their new reality with innate practicality and said, "There are already so many people in the world."

So George threw himself into his work and Valeria started to pursue a variety of causes, raising funds for international famine relief after natural disasters, and volunteering with programs that shipped medical supplies to third world countries for children in need.

It took some time to adjust to this new dimension of their life because it meant that Valeria accompanied George less frequently on his business travels.

At first, their prolonged absences from each other made them wonder, and worry, if they could sustain their relationship over distance and time, but they soon learned to trust that their fundamental connection would remain strong and solid even when they were apart for several months. In reality, the separation was often a blessing for their marriage because their strong personalities sometimes brought them into conflict. At those times, George felt that his wife was not always the easiest person to get along with, and Valeria found him to be similarly argumentative and stubborn. But they always managed to resolve their disagreements, and after a long separation, when they came together again, to their surprise they were always more in love than before.

As time went by, they found themselves wondering occasionally how life might have been different if they had had children of their own. Missing out on parenthood was perhaps their only regret—a rare, momentary shadow in an otherwise sunny existence.

George glanced with affection at his wife. He enjoyed watching her focused intently on the road.

Soon they came to the exit for Lugano and descended toward the lake, reaching the road that ran along its shore. The picture postcard view of the city with Monte Brè in the background always gave George a sense of serenity, and he was glad to be home.

A few minutes later, Valeria pulled into the cobblestone driveway of their house on the hillside overlooking the lake. George took in the scenery and was delighted to see that everything was as it always had been. Nothing had changed.

While Valeria fixed lunch for them, George unpacked quickly. He went into the kitchen alcove where she was setting the table and hugged her from behind.

"Mm," Valeria said, covering his hands with her own. "Give me a few minutes and we'll be ready. I just need to fix us a salad."

George headed into the living room where a large picture window provided a spectacular view of Lake Lugano. He played a CD of Beethoven's "Emperor Concerto" and sat in his favorite chair, emptying his mind to take in the music. It was time to relax, to think of nothing, or to imagine some future vacation.

The sound of clinking glasses at the table—Valeria filling them with sparkling water—roused him from his reverie.

"Did you doze off?" she asked.

"No. I was daydreaming. It was so intense that I could actually see the people and things I was thinking about."

"Ha! So now you're even clairvoyant! You know, nothing about you surprises me anymore!"

George protested good-humoredly as he joined her at the table, "You were the one who got me started years back. Ever since Dubai you've encouraged me to see beneath the surface of things and look at situations and people's behavior with different eyes. What do you want? I'm a 'big picture' guy and a fast learner."

"Yes, I know. Your insight and intelligence have always helped me to feel at ease with my own life. It's a rare thing for a woman of today to admit that 'if he says so, it must be true.' You've morally domesticated me."

"Oh, please!" George retorted in protest. "If anything, you're the one who's shaped my whole life with relentless, creative prodding. But I'm not complaining. Sometimes when I make decisions at work, things that you have no idea about, I find myself resorting to your theories, even your astrology notions, and wondering if you'd agree with what I'm doing."

Valeria's eyes twinkled with mischief, "Well, it's nice to hear that you actually follow my advice. Next you'll be asking me for directions when we go into town."

Later, they went for a walk. They left the house holding hands like a couple of carefree kids, but in truth, they were anything but carefree.

They had talked at other times, usually on the anniversaries of their parents' deaths, about how, once you reach a certain age, the happy-go-lucky spirit that fools you into thinking you're still in complete control of your surroundings is gone for good.

When your parents are no longer there to shelter and protect you, you realize that you're on the front lines now, alone and responsible for those following in your wake.

Valeria had pointed out to him that this was the reason why in the entrance to many homes in ancient Rome, there was a niche in the wall displaying statues of ancestors. People turned to their forebears for protection and comfort. They attempted to recreate that layer of parental protection in order to attain a feeling of temporary security.

As rational human beings who confronted reality honestly, George and Valeria were not given to fooling themselves. They were aware of their vulnerability and from time to time, their conversations reflected that understanding.

As they were climbing the path that led up the hill behind their house, George casually asked, "Have you decided yet if you can join me in China? I could use your help to keep Ryan on track. You know him better than I do. Perhaps your perspective on his 2012 obsession will calm him down."

"Oh, I don't imagine I have that kind of influence on him," Valeria said lightly.

"I'd really like you to come."

Valeria turned serious, "I'm trying to rearrange my schedule. Have you given any thought to my request?"

George glanced sideways at his wife. It was one of Valeria's peculiar qualities to change course in the middle of a conversation suddenly without warning, like a sailboat tacking in a different direction. With people who didn't know her, it often led to momentary misunderstandings, which were quite amusing. Even George felt at sea with her once in a while, but this time he knew exactly where she was headed and what she wanted to talk about—him pulling back from his business.

"Can't we discuss this some other time?" he pleaded. "I just got here, and I have a lot on my mind. I was hoping you'd help me forget it for a while."

"There never seems to be a good time," Valeria said accusingly.

They walked in tense silence for a while until they reached a wooden bench by a lookout. George stopped and said, "When I've wrapped up this China project, we can continue this discussion. I promise."

Valeria looked into his eyes. "I'll hold you to that."

"I know you will."

They sat down, engrossed in their own thoughts. The beautiful view of the lake did nothing to lighten the melancholic atmosphere that had descended on them.

It was Valeria who broke the mood by returning to their previous subject.

"So tell me about Ryan's newfangled ideas."

George, grateful for the lifeline she had thrown him, started in eagerly. "Well, he gave me this book, which I finished during my flight here. It lays out all the predictions and circumstances about December 21, 2012 pretty clearly, but it comes across as the usual end-of-the-world nonsense, just to get people excited. You and I agree on what happens in the final episode of our lives on Earth, so this book doesn't scare me or drive me to desperation. I do find it curious, though. What do you think?" He added, "And why would Ryan get so preoccupied with it?"

Valeria looked intent. "I've done a little research of my own, but for now I don't really have any opinions on it. A while back I read a piece in a newspaper by a columnist who said that if the people who believe in this theory decided to sell off their worldly possessions for chicken feed and kick back and enjoy the last few years of their lives, he'd like to be the one to buy it all up. If he had that idea, I'm sure it's crossed Ryan's mind as well. It's the way he's wired. Myself, I don't go for this apocalypse stuff. If anything, I'm with the interpreters who suggest that 2012 might usher in a shift in consciousness. Perhaps people's ways of thinking and living might change, and there'll be a reduction of the world's population, or at least some control on its growth."

"These changes are part of the Earth's geological and human history. But coming up with a theory about how and when these changes will take place strikes me as somewhat pointless, even if the Maya had advanced ideas about astronomy and its influence on the world. I wouldn't want to go to the extreme of our global warming Nobel Prize winner, Al Gore, who took on an enormous task without any kind of preparation. He talked about climate change speeding up without knowing the true causes. He turned it into a Hollywood disaster movie to shock the public and to promote himself. "

"It is always interesting to talk about such events, though, because beyond fixing on a particular date, what matters is that important changes are taking place. It's like what occurred during the Roman Empire with the advent of a new, progressive religion that opposed belief in a pantheon of pagan gods led by Jupiter. These changes didn't take place overnight, so there isn't a particular date we can point to. But it doesn't make them any less real."

"Christ's words of love and compassion, coupled with the general ethos of his time in history, accelerated these changes. Too bad his words were used improperly and interpreted out of context. And just like that, today we're once again at a big fork in the road."

"Fortunately, we've got plenty of politicians to straighten things out for us!" George said.

"And a bunch of journalists and talking media heads to pontificate about it!" Valeria joined in, laughing.

"Yes, they've become so gossip-oriented and downright negative, I get the feeling that they're just filling up pages and airwaves in search of the most obscure theories to satisfy the publishers' and networks' desires to attract larger audiences."

Valeria chimed in, "Sometimes I think we're like the Roman spectators in the bleachers of the Colosseum, watching the gladiator contests. Even if they aren't physically cruel nowadays, the game is the same: to provide the masses with sensationalism that will keep people talking for days, distracting them from the reality of their humdrum lives.

Sometimes I feel sorry for the individual journalists who are driven like gladiators to fight with every means at their disposal in order to keep their jobs. They have to shock and uncover scoops regardless of anything of significance that's really happening in the world. It's actually quite sad that so many intelligent people are imprisoned by this game and impose their recklessness upon readers and viewers just to survive."

George said, "I think you're too kindhearted. I'm not sure they're all that smart or aware of their gilded cages. They're quite happy to jump at any opportunity to come off as serious and 'enlightened,' and to turn it into the usual media circus of silly sound bites. No doubt, 2012 will be another great opportunity for them to 'strut their stuff.' But what I'm really interested in understanding is what's behind these highly publicized affairs, which become the darlings of radio and TV pundits."

"You're right," Valeria said. "The world has become accustomed to such predictions, which have existed since the dawn of history. It's as if people are intent on ratcheting up tension and fear, so they can later relax and feel relieved when nothing comes to pass."

"Exactly," George chimed in. "It's as they say in Italy about the many rules the government and its functionaries put in place. It's like someone who places his penis on the table, decides to strike it with a hammer, and is overjoyed when he misses. Mankind is but a soup of bodies and spirits contorting and stirring themselves up, if only as an exercise to combat encroaching rheumatism and boredom."

Valeria laughed. "What a preposterous idea, though not all that far from the truth."

George grinned. "Heady stuff, eh?"

She nodded. "I'm glad you're in a good mood again. I like it when you're happy."

George took her hand, "You know, I get a big kick out of your interpretations, they always make me go back and re-examine my own. *Now* pretend you're oblivious to my Valeria addiction!"

"That's what you always say, you knucklehead."

"And what are you, some little lamb following the shepherd? That's pretty funny. But I wouldn't want you any different than you are. There was this TV show I saw once about medical statistics and the way people in relationships act. Apparently, couples that fight all the time but forget about it the next day tend to live longer."

Valeria's eyes danced wickedly, "You called me about that and said that if it were true, we'd always stay together, we'd touch eternity. Don't you remember? This isn't the onset of Alzheimer's, is it?"

"Call it dementia, or better yet, selective dementia! Of course, *repetita iuvant*, as they say in Latin. Repetition is useful. Actually, we repeat ourselves all the time, though maybe it's a good idea to go back sometimes and overhaul our theories. By the way, saying it in Latin almost makes it true. It's a language that provides a sense of importance. You believe what it says!"

"Quit teasing me about my respect for the classics, history and philosophy!" Valeria retorted.

George suddenly became serious again, "But what that television program said is really quite profound and true. We argue, thus we become eternal—which is more or less what Descartes said. And for us, that's truer than ever."

"Our lives together have for many years been made up of meetings, trips, absences, arguments and reconciliations, but we're still together, and I believe that we really do feel we can't do without each other. Don't you think this bond comes from a place and time far back and stretches far into the future? Is it really madness to use the adjective 'eternal,' or is it just a way to say what we feel in this limited life?"

He paused. They looked at each other and without any thought or hesitation, suddenly embraced and kissed like two lovers in the throes of first love.

Over the course of the following days, they spoke often of these theories—sometimes just because it entertained them to do so.

In Valeria's presence, George thought less and less about Ryan and felt greatly renewed, ready to tackle whatever challenges would present themselves.

By the time he left for China, Valeria had agreed to catch up with him when he had finished a series of meetings in the provinces and Beijing, and had settled back into his office in Shanghai.

ꙮ CHAPTER 5

When George met up with Ryan in Shanghai a week later, Ryan had amassed even more material about December 21, 2012, including many foreign language editions and magazine articles. He was eager to discuss the Italian book he had given to George and was disappointed that it provided no new information beyond what he knew already. George's relative lack of interest in the subject didn't seem to bother him, and he continued to bend his ear about all the ins and outs of various predictions and interpretations.

To George it became clear that deep down inside Ryan did not think the world would come to an end on that day. Ryan did, however, feel inclined to believe that major changes would take place for life on Earth. Further, just as Valeria had predicted, he believed that if someone were lucky enough to survive these changes and had put together a smart plan, he might go on to become unimaginably wealthy.

George relaxed a bit when he realized that at bottom Ryan was as materialistic as ever. Still, the incessant conversations about the Mayas and 2012 became tedious and irritating. George found himself creating excuses just to avoid contact with Ryan and was relieved when the power plant required his presence on-site, away from Shanghai.

George did try to keep tabs on him, though—he'd never considered Ryan a person he could trust blindly—and he felt ill at ease not knowing Ryan's final aims. George was interested in finishing the job, doing it well, and avoiding any snags or arguments with financiers, clients, governments and suppliers, and for that he needed Ryan's financial acumen. His own reputation for handling all the technical specs and bringing projects to a conclusion was what kept him in good standing with all the various interested parties, and he didn't need Ryan getting too distracted to hold up his end of the job. So he humored him from time to time and listened, feigning interest when necessary.

George was relieved when Valeria arrived. They had at their disposal a small but pleasant apartment not far from one of Shanghai's business centers. With its traffic and elevated trains, the city reminded George of New York or Chicago, only more frenetic. He often told others that Shanghai was like Manhattan on steroids. There were a number of major centers with big buildings. You thought you were downtown, but when you looked out the window, you could see another downtown a few miles away, and then another, and another.

The apartment was comfortable enough. What neither of them liked was that they had little contact with indigenous Chinese traditions and life. The area was a warren of international shops with big brand names and Western products. They had visited the obvious cultural attractions on previous visits—the Great Wall, the Terracotta Warriors, the Jiangnan Watertowns, and more—but they were more interested in how actual people lived.

George experienced this when he was on-site, where living conditions had not changed much over the centuries. He was amazed that there were still some homes with no running water, no toilets and earthen floors, conditions that in any Western town would be considered abject poverty, but in rural China were simply a way of life.

Valeria had found some people at the university who helped her in her studies of Buddhism and China's other spiritual ways of thinking. Although religion was officially still frowned upon by the Communist government, so long as its functionaries did not perceive it as a threat to their authority, they left well enough alone, and she appreciated the exchange of ideas. With her interest in astrology, she found the Chinese zodiac especially intriguing, and this time she wanted to explore what, if any, similarities existed between it and the prediction of the Mayan calendar.

Ryan found this new information fascinating. And while George had counted on Valeria's arrival making things easier with Ryan, he ended up being sorely disappointed. If anything, the research she had done since Lugano only fueled Ryan's obsession, and as the days passed, the talks with him about what would happen on December 21, 2012, the day of the winter solstice, grew increasingly intense.

With his technical mind, George considered solstices and equinoxes merely the mathematical consequences of two movements in sync with one another: the Earth revolving around the sun and the rotation of the Earth on its own axis. The second movement follows laws of precession, by which the angle of the axis changes. This cycle takes a long time to complete a 360-degree rotation. Beyond the precise astronomical calculations, there are also the astrological interpretations to consider, which are significantly older. In the past, these two branches of human knowledge were actually one. To this day, astronomers and astrologists make use of the same data, although the interpretations of that data are very different indeed.

George, however, was not just a technician. He was a design engineer with imagination, creativity and remarkable sensitivity. Although he had thought of astrology as a kind of game at first—something he could use to tease Valeria—as the years passed he became more and more convinced that there really was something in it that could be applied to real life. He had encountered too many instances in which the astrological signs of his colleagues and business contacts correlated with their behavior, work styles, characters and ways of looking at the world to simply dismiss the theories of astrologers. He had reached the point of actually asking people who he interviewed or worked with what sign they had been born under in a half-joking, casual way, in order to treat them appropriately in terms of their personalities or the tasks he assigned them.

Each day he had proof of this, even in himself. He was a typical Sagittarius—adaptable, freedom loving, open to new ideas and experiences, interested in travel and philosophy, forward-looking and optimistic. The downside was a tendency toward arrogance and dogmatism, qualities which he had learned to suppress somewhat in his dealings with others.

Surely everyone tried, as he himself did, to employ different ways of thinking in order to improve and counter some of his predispositions, but the impulses that underlie and continue to influence and guide human minds were very strong, indeed. Celestial bodies exert a certain influence not only on the tides, seasons and climate, but on humans as well.

If this were true for individuals, then why shouldn't the movement of the sun and its planets in relation to the zodiac have a certain influence on mankind as a whole? This reasoning was based only on the result of combinations of movements and positions perceived by an earthbound subject looking toward the sky, thus making it a very limited, empirical science.

George was no expert in astronomy, a discipline which seemed to be evolving more and more quickly in recent years, much less an expert in astrology. He often deferred to Valeria when he needed more specific information and analysis regarding a particular case, and he was no longer amazed when almost every time he applied these theories to real life, they were confirmed.

Similarly, the research on 2012 that Valeria had done since their conversations in Lugano suggested that perhaps there truly was something to the predictions. George had the feeling that some kind of change really was in the air. He'd read up on the history of the Mayan calendar and the religious beliefs of ancient Egyptians, and then brushed up on various other prophesies, including those of Nostradamus. However, two upcoming events in particular attracted his attention: one astrological and the other astronomical. Both phenomena would occur together in 2012.

One would happen in spring when the sun would move through a new constellation, and instead of rising in Pisces, it would ascend in Aquarius. From our point of view on Earth, it takes the sun approximately 2,160 years to cross each of the 12 constellations of the zodiac as it travels backward through them. We call this the precession of the equinoxes and surprisingly, it is the basis of our calendar, even if we mark time in smaller segments as we go through each day. Of course, the 12 constellations were also mapped out by humans as they lifted their gaze toward the sky and recorded the formations of groups of stars for their own personal use. The 2,160-year cycle now finishing began around the time of the birth of Christ and is known as the Age of Pisces. Surely, it is no accident that images of fish appear prominently in Christian symbolism, and we still see them reproduced and used to this day.

The second event, which will occur during the 2012 winter solstice, is a rare galactic alignment, one that occurs only once every 25,625 years. The sun, Earth and other planets of our solar system will line up with the black hole at the center of our galaxy. At the same time, the Earth will complete the 360-degree rotation on its own axis, which happens only once every 25,920 years.

This astonishing conflation of events on December 21 has given rise to a host of theories and prophecies, including the predictions of the Mayan calendar, which comes to an end at about the same time that the world must find a new equilibrium. Perhaps it isn't just by chance that the Woman of the Apocalypse in the Book of Revelation is dressed in pure sunlight with the moon beneath her feet, wearing a crown of 12 stars, which coincides with the number of constellations in the zodiac.

For George, a man with his feet planted firmly on the ground despite his interest in astrology, who in his consideration of the universe asked only a few simple questions, the most practical expectation was that on December 21, 2012 we'll all enter definitively into the Age of Aquarius. Such a transition might bestow on man a new period of renewed energy and help to open our minds. This theory was held by various thinkers who reminded us that it was during the previous Age of Aquarius—some 26,000 years ago—that Cro-Magnon man evolved. At this particular moment in history, many signs point to a similar change in consciousness approaching.

George and Valeria had debated on several occasions if this were the result of celestial influence, or simply the cyclical nature of history as postulated by the Italian philosopher Giambattista Vico's "corsi e ricorsi storici." There is no simple and elegant formulation in English for this concept, although "ebb and flow" or "occurrence and recurrence of history" come close.

It must certainly be true that, for reasons unknown, at least at first glance, the way people think about their place in the world proceeds along a slow, undulatory path, with long periods of almost imperceptible changes that at some point appear to gain speed and go to extremes, like a wave that has traveled for thousands of miles approaching land, finally cresting and crashing down on the beach.

That is the way progress occurs in the world. Ideas always spring from those individuals who, when it comes down to it, are responsible for either progress or regression in the world. The majority of them—and this goes especially for the politicians—think only of daily survival. And for them, ideas seem to be in hiding, as if in hibernation, but the ideas turn into reality in spite of them. A recent example is the Arab spring that blossomed across the Middle East from Libya to Egypt to Syria, in the name of freedom from oppressive regimes and ruling elites; although it remains to be seen if the upheavals will ultimately lead to a better understanding of life's value or simply to a change in regime.

The difficult thing to explain is why at a certain point, in a certain era, these ideas start to spark people's imaginations and spread widely.

The fact that they are often distorted and abused as they proliferate only speaks further to their power. Those who wish to gain possession over others in order to control them and exploit them play on the incredible force that emotion exercises over people, touching them in the deepest reaches of their "soul." That is to say, that place within where reason wields no absolute power, where a series of sensations later transformed into intuition roam freely within the self. The German philosopher, Immanuel Kant, dubbed them a priori forms that are universal and necessary.

George often thought of the quote on Kant's tombstone, which had so impressed him the first time he read it that he committed it to memory in the original German:

Zwei Dinge erfüllen das Gemüt mit immer neuer und zunehmender Bewunderung und Ehrfurcht, je öfter und anhaltender sich das Nachdenken damit beschäftigt: der bestirnte Himmel über mir und das moralische Gesetz in mir.

Two things fill the mind with ever new and increasing admiration and awe, the more often and intensely we reflect upon them: the starry heavens above me and the moral law within me.

In penetrating such a thought, one has the sensation of being a hopeless speck in an immense black hole. Then again, one might imagine passing through that black hole and finding the connection between the universe and the moral law hidden within us. However, moral law is not always a precise abstract entity. It is perhaps influenced by years of intuition that form a culture which in some way remains fastened to the species known as man.

George felt a shiver run down his spine, as during an epiphany when we think we have discovered something that smacks of the ineffable, yet is quite simple—something that lay before our eyes the whole time, but we never noticed.

"Do the star-studded heavens actually have something to do with these waves of human thought and life?" he mused.

When it came down to it, as Kant put it, both thought and life share this rapport with the incomprehensible, the inexplicable that sparks the admiration of anyone who tries to penetrate the secret of our existence with conventional reasoning, what we call rational thought.

At this point it strikes us: What are the limits of thought? When will thought actually overcome itself? Perhaps the old empirical theory that was based for many years on astrological interpretations contains some truth and does govern the tides that have generated the waves of such thoroughly widespread ideas.

⚮ CHAPTER 6

Despite all the discussions, time moved on. Christmas came and went with small celebrations leading up to a large party that would bring 2011 to an end and ring in 2012. Valeria, George, Ryan and Betty, Ryan's companion of the moment, attended a New Year's Eve gathering hosted by a large American corporation with offices in Shanghai. With the clouds of recession looming over the world economy, and the American economy in particular, there wasn't much to celebrate—save the hope for a better year to come.

Ryan showed no interest in the lively party, the extravagant food or the free-flowing champagne. Contrary to his usual gregarious self, that night he was extremely irritable. Valeria and George wondered whether it was due to the financial difficulties that weighed so heavily upon everyone at the time, but usually Ryan did not appear too concerned about all of that. He knew how to adapt to the system. It had to be something more deeply rooted.

The problem didn't appear to be Betty, whom he'd been seeing for just a few months. She was attractive, pleasant and fun to be with. There was no great commitment on either side, since she had her own interests and her job as a translator. George and Valeria imagined that the relationship would end when Ryan packed up to leave. They didn't see one another all that often now, just enough to keep loneliness at bay—two Americans lost in China.

Around one a.m., after the obligatory New Year's cheers, kisses and toasts, when the party was just beginning to lose steam, Ryan, with a very serious air about him, posed a question to their small group, "Do you all realize that we have less than a year to come up with a solution that will guarantee our safety after December 21, 2012? We're all intelligent people; we've got to take advantage of this situation."

"You must have just seen that movie, *2012*, again," George teased in an effort to lighten Ryan's mood. "All those special effects were pretty impressive, but come on, that's just kid's stuff. Those kinds of movies stir people up for a while, but when they leave the theater, they're happy to go eat a pizza and return to their normal lives. That kind of shock entertainment has been going on for thousands of years. In ancient times there were stories of gods and goddesses, and the people who either received their protection or were victims of their wrath. Today it's all this high-tech bamboozling that saves the heroes and damns the villains."

Ryan snapped back in a burst of excitement, "That has nothing to do with what's happening! Something's going on. With technology and all the knowledge we have, teamed up with fertile minds, we can dig up pretty exact indications of what's going to happen and how to survive these changes—and not just survive, but make a bundle in the process."

With her customary calm and lucidity, Valeria broke in, "First, explain to me what you mean by 'make a bundle.' If everything changes, what kind of conditions will exist that affords you the opportunity of living the high life? After all, isn't that what money is for? To buy or gobble up the things that make life comfortable and interesting? To gain the power to control the people around you? You know, there are other kinds of success in this world, a whole range of pleasures and activities. They may be things, passions, ideas, lifestyles, ways of communicating—or sharing with others. The list goes on and on."

She became more intense. "In the wake of this supposed catastrophe, what will attaining personal satisfaction really mean? Can you tell already, or at least imagine it? Why does making as much money as possible have to be the starting point?"

"Do you honestly think," asked Ryan heatedly, "that mankind is ever going to change all the defects and the very few virtues we have? The history of humanity is nothing but a slapping together of idiotic presumptions that pits everybody against everybody else in an ongoing quest for dominance through the conditioning of minds and the control of goods and services. It hasn't changed for thousands of years, and it never will!"

"The world's population will continue to balloon because one race or religion wants to dominate all the rest. This competition will only lead to huge catastrophes that give the world a chance to survive and move forward with so-called new ideas. But when you look at history, they're actually ideas that have already been used, abused, rendered obsolete and abandoned. What do you think, that all this much-touted globalization is going to lead mankind to a world that is unified and functional?"

"The way things are going, no, I don't think so," Valeria said.

"You see, people talk about globalization, but the bottom line is that everybody's waging their own finance wars, especially in the developing countries, not giving a damn about the conditions of average people who are barely able to survive. They suffer, they curse their lot, but mostly they reproduce, exponentially. Then what happens? Disenfranchised, stripped of their own culture, intoxicated by what they see around them on television and the Internet, they become unruly, seek out new horizons, and migrate, creating further confusion. "

"But it's always been this way," Valeria interjected. "The most documented example, and the one closest to us, is the history of Rome and its integration with the barbarian tribes."

"Which led to the Middle Ages—the Dark Ages. I may not be a history buff like you, Valeria, but that much I do know, thank you!"

"Then if you take a good look at this turn of events, you'll see I'm right," Valeria insisted, refusing to be shaken. "The values of the Middle Ages were completely different from the values of the Roman Empire. By changing the rules of the game and the opportunities available, a successful Roman man or woman would have needed more than a single lifetime to adapt and figure out how to eke out a miserable living in medieval times. If something like that happened now, what would you do with all your accumulated wealth? Stocks? Money? Land? Real estate? Factories? How would you defend it all?"

Ryan laughed disagreeably and said, "Well, look here, I've never seen Valeria so pessimistic. I don't think everything's going to change so drastically, like in the movies. The stock market would most likely grind to a halt for a while, but gold and other assets would continue to hold their value, as would land, especially if it could be used for agriculture. Industries would still have to produce the necessary goods, and there'd be trade, which would be worth even more. Everything would have to be confined to safe locations, and it would all regain value, which would make whomever owned it pretty damn powerful."

"Until desperate mobs show up at your door and snatch it all away from you," Valeria hissed.

George, who had been watching the argument heat up, piped up, "Well, if you have the means, you could always hire mercenaries, forge alliances, and spread out your sources of income in a bunch of different sectors and locations."

But Valeria was not to be deterred. She fixed her penetrating gaze on Ryan and said. "Here's a question you might ask yourself: A man like you, accustomed to leading a very comfortable life, aided by a bogus system like that of high finance—how would you ever get along in such a situation?"

Ryan was about to lash out with another comeback when Betty put her hand on his arm. A practical woman who had a knack for ignoring Ryan's occasional rants, she said, "Let's go take a walk around the tables and say hi to people we haven't talked to before they leave. I could use a little distraction, and so could you. The party's going to be over soon anyway."

For a moment it looked like Ryan would explode, but then he grinned and reasserted his charming façade. He mock-bowed to Valeria and let Betty take him by the hand, pull him up out of his chair and head for a table across the room.

George sat in silence next to Valeria. Then he smiled at her and said, "Penny for your thoughts?"

Valeria seemed to come out of a trance of her own. "I have no idea what got into me," she said, a curious expression on her face. "It's been a long time since I let Ryan get under my skin."

⚒ CHAPTER 7

It was still early in the year 2012, mid-February, and George's project was winding to a close. On this particular day he didn't have a whole lot to do, so he headed home early. He remembered the promise he'd made Valeria in Lugano to talk seriously about plans for their future. If there was one good thing to come of Ryan's continuous agitating regarding the coming "apocalypse," it was that it triggered George to give some thought to how he wanted to live his life.

While Ryan had continued badgering George, he had avoided any further discussion with Valeria—she had more of an influence on him than he'd like to admit, and her words on New Year's Eve had given him pause. Instead, he kept suggesting new schemes for a prosperous, safe future in the Age of Aquarius, when everything would change, and change in a hurry.

For his part, George had pored over enough books to begin constructing a theory of his own regarding what might be some sensible choices to make for life in the post-2012 era. The whole subject had a surprisingly stimulating influence on George—for the first time in his life he considered his future in more concrete terms. Up till now his mind had always been focused on his work, his relationship with Valeria and various short-term plans. He had hardly realized how many years had passed pursuing such a routine—although his life was anything but routine. In reality, one new adventure after another had kept him fully engaged and hadn't given him an opportunity to take notice of time slipping away.

The same was true for Valeria and her busy life. Both of them sincerely felt that they were still young. Their active lifestyles and their desire to keep learning new things had made them forget that they were getting older and that their bodies' limitations were growing, however imperceptibly.

When George stopped and thought about it, he realized he was growing tired of living out of suitcases in different hotel rooms and rental apartments across the globe, leading a nomadic existence with all the attendant inconveniences that usually only young people in pursuit of careers are obliged to put up with.

Unlike Ryan, George thought that if 2012 really did usher in some great catastrophe, he'd be better off savoring the pleasures of life now, and enjoying the company of people who appreciate stimulating relationships while it was still possible. He also wanted to expand his knowledge of this world, even if it served him no particular purpose. It was just out of curiosity—but curiosity is the child of an active intelligence and requires constant nourishment.

Since that New Year's Eve argument, relations between the two men had taken on a discordant aspect. Ryan sought to exploit George's scientific knowledge in order to clear up any doubts he had about the variously predicted coming disasters—shifts of the continents, the potential reversal of the magnetic field, the chances of a meteorite striking our planet, or of another celestial body approaching in close proximity to the Earth—and the outcome any of these occurrences might have on life as we know it.

He also tried to impose on George's friendships with others to help him make as much money in as short a time as possible to buy whatever he thought would guarantee him a more secure future. Nothing interested him more than chasing down as many deals as he could to get rich and, if possible, leave the hedge fund he worked for so he could be free to do whatever he wanted.

He pestered George so relentlessly and at times was so overbearing, that he became absolutely intolerable.

Ryan thought only of himself. And truly, he had only one person's needs to look after—his own. His parents had long since passed away, and he had divorced many years previously, ending a marriage that had lasted barely four years. He had provided his wife and their two children with what he believed was a sufficient settlement, which they used to begin a new life without him. The three of them spoke to Ryan only once a year, at Christmastime. Indeed, they wondered why Ryan bothered to make that annual call at all, considering that it was always as cool and formal as if they were distant acquaintances. And that was, in fact, what they had become; but Ryan always felt gratified afterwards, as if he had done his rightful duty.

That afternoon, Ryan's incessant chatter and tenacious pursuit of his single-minded obsession had finally gotten to George. Ryan had shaken his concentration and, most of all, undermined his serenity. Before leaving the office, George had come close to yelling at him— which was something he never did.

He'd raised his voice and said forcefully, "If the whole world goes down the drain, then let's at least be cheerful as we go and enjoy these last few moments while we can. Just quit pestering me with all your wacko ideas and let me work in peace! No, I'll tell you what: I'm out of here for the rest of the afternoon. And don't try to call me at home because I won't answer!"

With that tirade George stormed out the door. In the car, George called Valeria to tell her he was on his way and would be getting home in half an hour—neither of them liked surprises.

He realized that Ryan belonged to the category of people he would do best to avoid if the world really were coming to an end. His was an extreme case, but the example was so unmistakable—after all, he was not a fool, but an intelligent man—that it allowed George to see his own situation more clearly and reach a conclusion.

George was glad to find Valeria at the apartment. He wanted to relax and simply take in the calmness and depth of her spirit. He wanted to talk at length and be listened to, after being an unwilling sounding board for all the prattle that Ryan had inflicted on him.

If Valeria were curious about his early arrival home, she didn't show it. She made George a cup of tea and sat next to him on the sofa.

"You know," he said once he'd taken a sip, "in some way, Ryan has expanded upon your analysis of the Middle Ages. Now he's bent on trying to figure out the ideal place to be on December 21—the safest spot in order to stay as far away from the coming catastrophe as possible. And once he's done that, he says he'll try to figure out how he can keep living a comfortable life, and what he'll have to do, wherever he is, in order to achieve that."

"That's really absurd," replied Valeria. "Ryan has so much free time and so little personal satisfaction, he's taken to wasting all his energy on this. It's going to drive him crazy."

"He's driving me crazy already," George sighed. "Yet in a certain sense, he's helping me," he continued more animatedly. "He's got me so wrapped up in this imminent upheaval of the world that I've begun thinking the whole thing out."

Valeria drew near him with a heartening look and caressed his head. "That's something I'd never expect from you and your wide-ranging scientific mind."

"Well, what if by chance something really does happen?" George continued. "Maybe not some huge, catastrophic disaster, but just an enormous crisis. Why not take advantage of the little time left to do what we've always dreamed of doing? At least we'd go down, or even die, happy."

Valeria suddenly became serious. "Are you saying what I think you're saying?"

George looked at her steadily. "Yes, I am."

All at once, Valeria burst out laughing. "I can't believe it! At last! Hallelujah! It's taken the end of the world to get you to figure out that there's more to life than work. I have to remember to thank Ryan."

"Valeria, I want your help with this," George went on soberly. "Just like when we first met and you taught me how to travel the world for the sake of pure enjoyment. Let's talk it over. Let's make a plan. Let's make a goal for ourselves. We could devise a whole new outlook, say, by the end of the month, and then begin acting on it."

Valeria was barely able to contain her excitement, but having thought about this moment for some time, she gave a measured response.

"I think the first thing we have to do is stop giving ourselves deadlines. Sure, we'll talk about it. We'll relish the possibility of some cataclysmic change. If it happens, it happens."

"But what about my work?" George asked as if amazed.

"That will be the only thing I'll let you put a deadline on. Decide on the day—and make it as soon as possible—when you can pass your projects onto the members of your office staff, and then make it happen. Yes, as soon as you can, so the transition goes smoothly. From then on, all you'll do is consult—give them advice—if they need it.

After all these years of working together, you must have someone who can take up the reins. Come on, decide on the day—right now! Then we'll just let everything run its course."

"What do you mean, 'right now'?! How am I supposed to do that?"

"Now means now! Before dinner," Valeria urged. "Come on. Let's go! Then we'll head out to celebrate and drink the best wine we can find. So do it now!"

As George sat there, astonished, Valeria went into the other room. She soon returned carrying two glasses and a bottle of champagne.

"Give me a date and I'll uncork this," she insisted.

"I can't just up and leave everything. I have to think it over."

"Okay. I'll give you an extension. I'll fix us a snack, uncork the champagne, pour it into our glasses, and we'll sip it slowly to really savor it. And when the bottle's finished, the oracle will speak."

From his amazement, George slipped into a strange state of apparent bewilderment. When Valeria returned with a tray of sliced cheeses and crackers, he took his glass and drank. Valeria noticed how his eyes began to dart about the room, an expression of his roused interest, and how his cheeks reddened, always a sign of intense mental activity.

Fifteen minutes or so passed, during which time they toasted, munched on their snacks, laughed, and made a few irrelevant remarks.

Finally, George slumped back on the couch and said in nearly a whisper, "You're right. You're absolutely right. Two months from today, on the dot! All my current projects will be finished by then, and I won't take on anything new. Tomorrow I'll put out the word that I'll no longer be directly involved. In two months' time I'll be free."

He pronounced these words calmly, but there was determination in his tone—and a big smile on his face.

And thanks to the possible end of the world, Valeria felt exhilarated. She snuggled up to George and rested her head on his shoulder, unable to stop grinning. They sat like that for some time, in the contented afterglow of knowing that they had just crossed a momentous threshold in their life together.

Valeria was pleased beyond words. She had her own ideas regarding December 21, 2012, very different from Ryan's. She would tell George all about them when she thought the moment was right.

🐾 CHAPTER 8

The news that George was, at least partially, withdrawing from work at the end of his current project traveled around the world, literally—from China, where he was at the moment, to Japan, the United States, France, Switzerland, Dubai, Africa, Singapore and beyond. No one would have imagined that this dynamo of the engineering world would ever willingly go into early semi-retirement. Many of his colleagues were simply amazed and said so. Others called, concerned that there was something wrong. When they realized that that was not the case, they wished him all the best. George knew that some were even happy to see him go, in the spirit of "the king is dead, long live the king," because it meant there would be greater opportunities for them.

Determined that his firm and its clients should not have to worry about the future without him, George put in a tremendous amount of work prior to his departure to make sure he left everything in good shape, at least for the next few years. After that, who could provide any guarantees? In reality, no one believed that George would wind up on some mountainside, living the life of a hermit, or as a globetrotter, enjoying traveling the world. They assumed he'd always be involved with his engineering company in one way or another, in the capacity of a hands-on consultant.

Thus, after the initial flurry of news and gossip, things settled down within a few weeks. In the world of creative endeavors, there's no place for hysteria.

That was not the case for Ryan. His way of looking at things was like the special effects in movies—arousing emotions, blowing things out of proportion, and signaling a state of alarm.

"What's really behind George's decision?" he pondered.

He had discussed December 21 with George at length, clearly expressing all of his concerns and letting him in on his plans for surviving the possible calamity. From their New Years' Eve quarrel, Ryan had realized that Valeria was also conversant with the subject. This confirmed what he had known about her for some time: that she was capable of profound thought and insights. What was she keeping from him that she was sharing with George? He had to find out.

Ryan's first move was to meet with George. He wanted to express his bewilderment over the decision to hand over the day-to-day operations of his business and ask George why he had not first shared the news with him, his friend, before releasing it officially. Ryan scheduled an appointment and met George in his office with the excuse of needing to clear up a few things regarding work matters.

George had come home late the night before from the project site. The extra hours he was putting in had taken their toll. He looked tired, as was to be expected, but the sense of well-being and calm emanating from him took Ryan aback.

Covering his surprise, he flashed a vulpine grin, shook George's hand, hugged him and said, "I can't believe a workaholic like you wants to take such a long vacation!"

As George was about to reply, Ryan went on quickly, "Don't tell me you mean to go into semi-retirement. Sometimes we get tired, dream of a different life, but...you can't teach an old dog new tricks."

George protested, "No, no, I'm serious about this. I want to enjoy some of the good things life has to offer, and that includes my relationship with Valeria."

Hearing Valeria's name, Ryan squinted slightly and searched George's eyes as he continued his fishing expedition in a somewhat hushed tone. "Ah, so Valeria's got something to do with this...I knew it! That wonderful woman convinced you. She's a rock for you, really. I'm happy for you—but only for the moment. You'll be back...you'll be back. Remember that."

"Oh, I agree with you there," George replied, "I'm not going to disappear. But as far as work goes, I have no intention of continuing at the frantic pace I've been going. Valeria's arguments were so convincing that I simply couldn't refuse."

Ryan shifted his gaze and sat down across from George, who now felt obliged to take a seat himself. Then Ryan handed him three sheets of paper listing a series of questions, all numbered.

"I'd appreciate if you'd have your staff answer these questions, so I can complete my financial report. The usual stuff and nonsense."

As George nodded and absentmindedly scanned the pages, Ryan smiled broadly and added, "What do you say to getting some lunch? I'm dying to hear what led up to your decision to quit."

George looked up, somewhat confused by Ryan's interest. "Weren't you the one a few months ago who said you needed a breather from work in order to think more about yourself, make more money, and prepare for what to do come December 21?"

"Maybe your idea was infectious...I want a new place to call home, a place where I feel comfortable and safe, together with Valeria, and stop living like a nomad, roaming all over the world. We've decided that our house in Lugano will be our permanent home. Anything wrong with that?"

"Definitely not," said Ryan, making a deliberate show of his approval of the decision.

"Listen," George said, "I'd love to do lunch, but we'll have to make it another time. I have to prepare for meetings this afternoon— tying up loose ends. You understand."

Ryan suspected George was just trying to get rid of him; he *had* acted somewhat distant over the past few weeks. Then again, he was understandably busy. In either case, Ryan was not going to let the opportunity slip by.

"No problem," he said. "I'm putting a couple of deals together that could be quite lucrative, and I wanted to offer you a piece of the action, but it can wait. I do want to see you and Valeria, though, before you 'make your escape.' Are you free Saturday evening?"

He fixed his eyes on George, who had never been a good liar, and continued quickly, "Why don't I come over? I promise I'll be on my best behavior, and I'll bring a bottle of your favorite wine."

And before George could reply, he quickly added, putting on a forlorn expression, "You can't deny me the opportunity to celebrate with you two."

George knew he could not refuse the offer, much as he wanted to, and so he nodded in agreement.

The appointed evening came and, much to Valeria and George's surprise, Ryan showed up with a bouquet of roses for the hostess and two very expensive bottles of wine, one white, chilled, and a red Barolo.

He handed the flowers to Valeria and guffawed, "Let's uncork this white in celebration of George's fantastic decision! Let's enjoy life to the fullest, especially with December looming on the horizon."

"Really, Ryan," Valeria said as she took the flowers into the kitchen to put in a vase with water, "You're making too much of this. It's just an opportunity for George to get a breath of fresh air and dedicate a little more time to me."

"I knew you had a hand in this," Ryan teased. "You'll never cease to amaze me."

After the initial toast as the three were settling into the living room chairs, Ryan pitched his opening gambit to delve into his friends' intimate sphere.

"Sooo…why Lugano? The world's such a big place and you two know so many wonderful spots. Why not some beautiful island in the Pacific, or…?"

Valeria smiled.

"Come on, clue me in…I'm very curious."

George eyed his guest and said, "I don't see why you're so surprised. Valeria was born in Lugano and I love being with her. I even have an office there, so if someone from the firm really needs to reach me–"

"Now, George…" Valeria teased indulgently. "No backsliding, you promised."

George squeezed her hand affectionately. "Not to worry, darling."

He turned to Ryan, "As far as the rest of the world—and those South Seas islands—we can visit them whenever we want. You know, during all these years of traipsing around, the house in Lugano has really always been our home. I think it's fairly logical, actually."

"I guess so," Ryan conceded, somewhat disappointed.

With a sly smile, Valeria observed Ryan's expressions in silence as he looked back and forth between George and her, struggling to make up his mind about how to proceed.

Ryan finally turned to her and, doing his best to hide his sense of urgency, casually said, "Talk about clamming up—and you of all people, the woman with a thousand explanations and theories! You can't tell me that's all there is to it. Why don't you humor me, say something that proves me right in thinking that your decision is based on concrete reasons that go beyond the ones I've heard so far? I really am curious to find out. I never would have imagined George winding down his days in Switzerland."

"What is it you want to know?" Valeria responded, getting up and heading into the kitchen.

She knew exactly why he'd gotten himself invited to dinner and had already figured where the topic of conversation would be headed. She had even warned George not to fall into Ryan's trap and encourage his crazy talk, much less answer his questions in a way that would stoke an endless discussion. George still had another month left to spend in Shanghai with Ryan and did not need to be dragged any further into his crazy theories and obsessions.

She knew Ryan all too well. If he believed some giant catastrophe was at hand, he'd also feel cocksure that he was going to come out on top when it occurred. And because he was always looking for an edge, he'd want to extract every bit of information he could from people he considered intelligent—deep, creative thinkers—and also practical enough to help devise a concrete, winning plan. Ryan did not possess those qualities, except when it came to capital investment and moving money around the world to increase his financial gain.

While Valeria refreshed the appetizer tray with savory tarts and cheeses, George and Ryan sat in silence. As soon as she returned, Ryan resumed his chatter.

"Oh, don't get me wrong, I don't want to cast any doubt on your decisions and the motivation behind them. It's just that I'm determined to overhaul my own life, as I told you, so I'm curious about understanding why someone else would want to do the same."

Valeria looked at him kindly. "You know, Ryan, after you've reached a certain age, the main goal is to find a place where you feel most comfortable. You seek serenity. And there's more than enough of that in Switzerland, if you've put aside enough money. And to fight off any boredom that might creep up on us, we can go to places in Italy and France where there are plenty of thrills and excitement. Then, when it gets too cold in winter, Malpensa airport is only an hour's drive away—from there we can fly anywhere we want, or visit our friends all over the world."

Ryan realized that he couldn't hope to make any progress on this front, and the evening continued with routine conversation about various travel experiences, people they'd met and the usual gossip. Now and then Ryan would allude to December 21, hoping to glean some insight into George and Valeria's decision—and by now he was certain she was the driving force behind it—only to see them evade that subject and turn to another.

Valeria sensed his mounting frustration. After dinner, she decided to share some of her ideas.

As they were relaxing over glasses of brandy, she turned to him and said, "After all the research I've done about the Mayan prophecies and the coming of the Age of Aquarius, I have come to the conclusion that the world is now moving toward a new way of thinking and acting. Of course, this will lead to huge practical problems, but won't mean the end of the world. On the contrary, people born under the sign of Aquarius tend to think of the future, they seek peace and they're very family oriented. Maybe the world will change for the better..."

"So where does that leave us? What can we do about it? Nothing. The Earth has seen many similar occurrences since the dawn of time, but humanity is still here hating and loving, reproducing, killing and helping one another, and all the rest."

"If you want my opinion: Relax. It won't be anything so dramatic that we can't live through and overcome it."

"But I've never gone through such an experience!" Ryan exclaimed heatedly.

"That doesn't matter a bit. The art of survival is in all of our DNA; it's been passed down to us for ages. When the time comes, you'll know exactly what to do."

"That's easy for you to say," Ryan retorted heatedly. "You and George have got it all figured out!"

After a pause, Valeria sighed. "Please, Ryan, can we not talk about this anymore? You're making a big to-do over nothing. History will take its course, and we will make our way through it. We can't do any more than that. Besides, nothing's going to happen."

Ryan raised his hands in acquiescence, "Okay."

But he felt alone and defeated. He was faced with a dilemma that haunted him. He believed with all his heart that it was real, but nobody seemed to take him seriously—not even Valeria, who, he was certain, knew a great deal more than she was willing to let on.

As the evening drew to a close, Ryan put up a good front, despite his frustration, and to all outward appearances, departed on friendly terms. But he was deeply dissatisfied and churning inside.

On the way home, he thought about how lucky his friend George was to have Valeria. Not for the first time, he considered that he might have made a mistake when he let her go.

CHAPTER 9

They had met in New York when they were both still in their 20s. Ryan was a rising star in the financial world, working for a large Wall Street firm. His wheeling and dealing on the stock market had paid generous dividends not only for his clients, but for himself, too. He had made some very advantageous trades on his own and achieved a certain degree of financial independence. He lived in a swanky apartment in a high-rise on the Upper East Side, ran with a crowd of wealthy and important people, and enjoyed the life of a successful yuppie, chasing after pretty young women and basking in his accomplishments. He had managed to come a long way from his early years in an impoverished family beset by constant money worries. His father always had his hands in some get-rich-quick scheme or other that never paid off, and his mother always supported him through thick and thin. Ryan was determined to do better at any cost.

One evening, at a party organized by the Swiss embassy—a stodgy, tedious affair, where conversation revolved around new models of international finance—he met a young woman who had recently arrived in New York. She wanted to further her knowledge about ancient Egypt and its religions, and was working with the curator of the Egyptian exhibit at the Metropolitan Museum of Art.

On first impression, Valeria wasn't a knockout, although she had a pretty face and pleasant disposition. But when she talked about her passion for Egyptology, she came alive. Her face became flushed and animated, her eyes flashed with brilliance, and she exuded an almost magnetic attraction. In addition, with her cultured, refined manners and European perspective—her father had been an Italian diplomat who had taken her on many of his travels—she was unlike anyone Ryan had ever met before, and he was intrigued.

For her part Valeria, although unprepared and a bit overwhelmed by the chaotic bustle of New York, was also thoroughly fascinated by the novelty of it all. She did not realize at first that much of the spirited life in the circles she frequented was superficial and based on appearances, glitz and wagging tongues.

Thus, it was not difficult for Ryan to attract her attention. He was handsome, charming and witty, the ideal representative of this brave new world that she found so enthralling.

At the beginning, pursuing Valeria was only a game of mild curiosity for Ryan. But he soon discovered how different she was from the American women he was used to spending time with. Her sensibility, intelligence and intuitive approach to different situations gave her a kind of power and allure, and he fell under her spell without quite knowing how it had happened.

At a certain point, he started to feel inferior to her, both in background and manners, which roused his competitive spirit. For a man like Ryan, Valeria presented a challenge. He had to prove to himself that he could make her fall in love with him, take her to bed and make her scream in ecstasy.

Conquering Valeria became a mission for him. He planned it with the same attention to detail he lavished on important financial transactions and pursued her with the same, dogged determination that made him successful in his business.

He wooed her with dinners, trips to the opera and visits to art galleries. He used his research abilities and contacts to put her in touch with people in academia that could further her studies and open doors she didn't know existed. He pretended to be curious about Egyptology himself. With his tremendous memory, it was easy for him to simulate a more than passing interest in psychology and spirituality, past and present.

Valeria enjoyed the attention and appreciated Ryan assisting her studies, but when it came to their relationship, she drew the line at little caresses and occasional kisses. It wasn't that she was prudish about sex. She simply didn't know about the unwritten American dating rule of going to bed with someone after the third date.

Ryan renewed his efforts. At parties and official functions, he always gave the impression to others that Valeria was the woman of his heart. It got to the point where his female friends figured he was engaged to her and no longer part of the singles scene.

At one of the parties, a former conquest teased him about finally falling in love. When Valeria overheard him saying, "Yes, she makes me feel like she's the one," she looked at him in a new light. The distance between being infatuated with Ryan and ending up in his bed was now just a short step.

One night, after a romantic dinner and plenty of wine, they went to his apartment and made love. Ryan used every technique he knew, relentless in his desire to arouse an intense passion in his partner. Finally, he made Valeria scream uncontrollably in the throes of love. For a fleeting moment he felt like a conqueror, satisfied with his well executed victory.

He was Ryan the Great, and Valeria, just like every other woman he had possessed, was merely a creature in heat.

He had no idea then that his arrogant judgment was the biggest mistake of his life.

And so their relationship continued. Valeria never asked herself what she saw for their future together. She was happy simply to let things develop between them, and enjoyed the fast life in New York with the joys and pleasure of sex with Ryan. Everything was going well. Switzerland was far away. What more could she want from life?

It was a new attitude on Ryan's part that slowly awakened her to a different reality. Satisfied with his victory, Ryan let his real personality come to the surface. For weeks, he had feigned an interest in Valeria and her pursuits. Gradually, he became indifferent, looking more and more like a person incapable of understanding the call of humanity, and disinterested in the basic problems other people experienced in everyday life. The fact that he was still fascinated by her didn't matter. If anything, it got in the way. Ryan was too immature to respect Valeria for it and unable to admit to himself that she had any power over him.

He continued to see Valeria, even considered marrying her. He told himself that it would be a calculated union. As far as he was concerned, they were good together. With her social poise, she would greatly benefit his career. He also figured that her background and relative wealth might be good for business, expanding his contacts "across the pond."

What he didn't count on was Valeria's sensitivity and perceptiveness. She quickly realized that Ryan took pleasure in humiliating others with little gestures, snide remarks and irritation when he did not get what he wanted right away. They had some spirited arguments when Valeria, refusing to let herself be controlled by him, spoke her mind in no uncertain terms.

For a while, she tried to rekindle the early fire of their relationship by being more sensitive to his needs, but she soon realized that Ryan was not about to change. She was not upset with him. She felt more angry with herself for having been so foolish and mistaken in her judgment as to not recognize who he was from the beginning. She also realized that she would never be able to act that way herself—had no interest in it—and that the high-flying, cutthroat world of international finance was not for her.

One evening when they were out to dinner, Ryan carried on with their conversation as if he had no real interest in the subject matter. In reality, he was testing his feelings of dissatisfaction and confusion in Valeria's presence, which had abated in time. He wished he could read her better, so he could feel in control.

At a certain moment, she said, "Ryan, the day after tomorrow I am leaving for Switzerland."

The simple statement struck him like a blow.

"But your program isn't finished for another month and a half," he sputtered.

"I know."

"Where is this coming from? Why do you want to leave me so suddenly?"

"Because my life in New York City and our relationship are over. You helped reveal to me intense feelings I didn't know I was capable of, and I thank you for that. Much as I'd like to change you, I'm not able to. We live in two different worlds."

The threat of abandonment brought out the stubbornness in Ryan. He tried everything in his power to dissuade her, but his every effort faltered in the face of Valeria's serene certainty.

In the end he consented.

Valeria kissed him on the cheek and said, "You are a fighter—I admire that in you. I am just a woman who thinks and tries to understand."

She did not say goodbye, and left the restaurant by herself.

Ryan stood there, furious because he had lost control of the situation, but also relieved and happy that it was over; Valeria had made him feel inferior, at times almost guilty. He couldn't admit to himself how humiliated he felt, so he contented himself with the thought, "I will use her for something when the time comes."

When Ryan became the manager of a large international hedge fund and started to travel to Europe, Asia and the Middle East, he occasionally ran into Valeria. The first time, there was some awkwardness, with Ryan acting as if what had happened between them did not matter to him. Valeria, whose intuition told her that he was still smarting from her rejection, appreciated his efforts to appear otherwise. In time, it got easier and they actually enjoyed each other's company for an occasional evening, reverting to the fun times they had had together when they first met, although they never were sexually involved again.

And when George showed up on the scene in Dubai and became involved with Valeria, Ryan encouraged them to draw closer whenever he could. He figured it would cement his business relations with George, whom he admired. And it did.

⚶ CHAPTER 10

By the time Ryan returned to his empty apartment in Shanghai, after his dinner with George and Valeria, he had reached a decision. Perhaps his matchmaking would pay dividends after all. Even if Valeria would not tell him all she knew, she would obviously save her husband come December, and so Ryan would follow them, copying their movements and actions in order to attain the same results—and survive the approaching cataclysm along with them.

As the day of George's departure from Shanghai drew near, he continued to be absorbed by the frantic pace of winding up his affairs. Preparing for such a change in lifestyle wasn't easy for a man with an overwhelming sense of responsibility. He made several quick trips to his company offices in the United States and Switzerland to make sure the transition was as seamless as possible. Valeria kept close by his side—she did not want to run the risk of him changing his mind or delaying his departure date. Any holdup might put the whole plan in jeopardy. She could hardly wait for the appointed day when George would step down as CEO from his firm for good.

At this point Valeria thanked her lucky stars for Ryan, whose incredible obsession over December 2012 had set the entire undertaking into motion. Living a truer, more serene life with her husband was something she'd been dreaming of for quite some time. Long before George, she had tired of hopping on airplanes every few days. Flying had become a cross to bear—with all the hassles involved in getting to the airport and coping with the confusion there, being herded like cows through all the security measures. Nor did Valeria enjoy creating places to call home all over the world, which offered none of the pleasures of a genuine domicile.

But while she was grateful to Ryan in her thoughts, she was relieved that he spent less and less actual time in George's company, opting instead to send someone from his staff to deal with business matters. Ryan was busy traveling to the various locations where his deals were in the making. He was convinced more than ever that he had to accumulate as much money and gold as he could, as well as control of companies that produced products essential for the future, and even farmland in key places throughout the world.

When he discovered that some of his colleagues were beginning to talk about him, wondering what he was up to, he paid no attention. His reputation was no longer a concern to him. He figured the future would be so altered, no one would care how he came by his fortune.

What tormented Ryan the most was not knowing where to establish his main place of residence. It irked him that he had not succeeded in figuring out why George and Valeria had chosen to settle in Lugano. There had to be something they knew that he didn't. He took pains to gather information on the pros and cons of the places he thought would be the safest with the same obsessive attitude he had demonstrated about the predictions regarding 2012.

He wanted to avoid areas with active volcanoes, places subject to earthquakes, low-lying coastal zones, plains and deserts. Most of all, he wanted to stay as far as he could from the North and South Poles and the equator.

As he worked all of this out, it dawned on him that perhaps George and Valeria had set their minds on Switzerland for those very same reasons. After all, George was an expert on the geological problems inherent to each continent, having worked on construction projects all over the world.

The Alps had formed when the African continent collided with the European continent. Then, in the process of shifting southward, Africa left one of its sections attached to Europe, an area that included practically everything south of the Alps. This meant that the mountains that had once marked the borderline between the two continents, which is to say, the Alps, were so solid that Africa broke in two as it withdrew from them.

What's more, over the centuries Switzerland had always remained in some way protected against the great invasions, being surrounded and divided by high, impenetrable mountains, making it difficult to conquer, unify or control.

Whenever other tribes or nations tried, after the upheaval created by the invaders had abated, everything went back to the way it had been before. Even today, Switzerland retained much of its protected singularity: It lay in the heart of Europe, yet did not belong to the European Union; it was divided into four cantons that each spoke its own language; and it maintained its independence and high standard of living.

Ryan remembered how at a party in a colleague's living room in Zurich, someone had asked how Switzerland could ever be regarded as a single nation, and one so well defined and compact at that, considering its different cantons, languages, affiliations and cultures. The teenage daughter of the host, one of those precocious youngsters who seem to be too smart for their own good, had quipped, "That's easy. They all worship the same god: money." Everyone had laughed and nodded thoughtfully. The girl had hit the nail on the head. Blessed is the frankness of youth.

"That's it, then," Ryan said to himself. "My search is over. I'll buy a house near Lugano. I'll do it discreetly, and I won't say a thing to George and Valeria."

He knew that buying a home in Switzerland and establishing residency there would be complicated, but with the help of friends and the money he had at his disposal, it shouldn't prove to be impossible. He'd also look for some vacant land in Switzerland or in nearby Italy or France where he could raise livestock and do some farming, if necessary.

"Yes!" he exclaimed. "Now I've got a plan! George and Valeria, we'll reunite after December 21, 2012…and then we'll see who's played their cards best!"

PART

II

🐚 CHAPTER 11

December 21, 2012 came and went.

As George had predicted, nothing happened.

By then, he and Valeria were happily ensconced in their beautiful home in Lugano and adjusting to their new life together, far removed from the daily demands of George's business.

George was now truly semi-retired and freely admitted that Valeria had been right in telling him how much he would appreciate his new consulting role. He could handle it with gusto and creativity and not have to worry about the mundane day-to-day matters, which had always been irritating and taxing of his time and energy.

For the past two months, he and Valeria had been doing their best to dodge the media frenzy leading up to the fateful day, although it was nearly impossible not to hear some report or yet another conjecture about the events surrounding that year's winter solstice and its possible effects. Newly minted experts had sprung up overnight. Theories abounded.

There were basically two camps: one focusing on physical explanations, the other on mystical prophecies. In the first camp, some were catastrophic, forecasting radical climate change, others predicted a shift in the Earth's magnetic field or tilt in the Earth's axis along with dire consequences. Then there were those who warned of a total breakdown in electronic communication and devices using wireless technology.

It was perhaps not surprising that a considerable number of people welcomed a world without e-mail and text messaging, but most who bought into that theory were panic-stricken and sought alternatives in desperate fashion. Post offices and freight companies saw a spike in their customer base.

The spokespeople for the other, more "mystical" camp touted a change in our perception of life's problems, which would open the door to a new era of spiritual relations among mankind, the universe and the Divine. The most extreme adherents were determined to usher in the new age with celebrations across the globe. Travel companies got in on the action, offering trips to spiritual locations throughout the world, from Stonehenge in England, to Angkor Wat in Cambodia, Machu Picchu in Peru, and the great pyramids in Egypt. A special pilgrimage to Chichen Itza, the ancient Mayan religious center in the Yucatan, brought tens of thousands of visitors, boosting the local economy, but also creating traffic jams and causing housing and food shortages in the area.

In all their diversity, the various theories did share one thing— the certainty that time was up for the current operational frameworks, and that there was a need for a new enlightenment that would save humanity and the planet. Otherwise, life as we knew it would disappear altogether. Perhaps a new embryonic development would usher in a brand new cycle, a long period of evolution, as happened millions of years ago. Indeed, mankind had been itching for this for quite a few years now.

For George and Valeria, who watched all the hullabaloo and media hubbub from the sidelines with some amusement, none of it represented anything new. Their studies had taught them that the history of the world was chock full of similar moments.

George, in one of his early arguments with Ryan, when he was still trying to persuade him to give up his obsession with 2012, had mentioned the best known example: Jesus Christ's words of love, forgiveness and humility.

"It really doesn't matter who Christ was, we can leave that to the experts," he had said. "What's important is the fact that the world was waiting for that message, and that the world adopted it and betrayed it as it sought to apply and interpret Christ's teachings. Oh, that message is still valid today, but it has been so misinterpreted and watered down that it has been drained of all its force. The same may be said of other messages that came to the fore in other parts of the world and were abused by the vast majority."

He had gotten quite philosophical about it. "Day in and day out, mankind's reason has created laws, beliefs and a model of life that today are in crisis. And the crisis infuses each day with greater and greater urgency, as there seems to be less and less time remaining to come up with a possible remedy. The speed of the electronic world, the growth of populations and their needs, the empty promises of governments, and the incapacity of humanity to embrace these pressing developments rationally has led us to create radical and fanciful solutions in response to our frustrations. What's more, disturbances created by climatic anomalies and solar radiation, volcanic eruptions, earthquakes and tsunamis, albeit explicable, only contribute to feeding the fire of people's anxieties and lead them to come up with far-fetched, fantastic predictions."

"Believe me, Ryan, this phenomenon has been repeated over and over again at different times and in different areas of the world, followed by periods of confusion, decay and mass extinction."

Needless to say, Ryan had not shown the least bit of interest in George's analysis—it was not what he wanted to hear—and had continued his fanatical pursuit of the Mayan theories as interpreted by the modern world.

At the time, George had been extremely frustrated, but in retrospect, he realized that conversation had been one of the triggers that led him to consider making a fundamental change in his life. And for that he was grateful, because his relationship with Valeria had deepened in ways he could not have imagined.

 CHAPTER 12

For Ryan, the lead-up to December 21 and its passing without any significant change whatsoever was disappointing to say the least. He had moved to Lugano, unbeknownst to George and Valeria, to a secluded mansion surrounded by high protective walls. He had outfitted it with the most up-to-date security measures and stocked up on food and supplies like a medieval warlord preparing for a siege.

From his protected "castle," he had followed the newscasts and discussions with the same fervent intensity that he had devoted to his initial research. He had executed all his plans with considerable success, amassing wealth and resources. He had eagerly anticipated news of some disaster or doom, and nothing had happened.

But he wasn't ready to give up on what he had labored for so compulsively. He was as certain as ever that George had withdrawn from his company for a more serious reason than he had shared, and that Valeria had been deliberately mysterious, withholding essential knowledge that she had. If anyone knew what was what, it would be them.

It was the afternoon of December 23. Valeria and George were busy getting their home ready for a Christmas Eve get-together with close friends. Much as they had avoided the media circus, they couldn't help talking about the aftermath and the letdown all the people who had expected cataclysmic events must be experiencing.

Valeria, coming out of the kitchen with a sprig of mistletoe to hang above the entryway into the living room, said to George, "I'd like to know just what all those people who offered to buy up property and valuables at cut-rate prices prior to the 'catastrophe' actually managed to get their hands on, and how many gullible souls got suckered in. I can't help wondering how Ryan is doing considering how obsessed he was with it all."

"No doubt, one day he'll be back to pester us with something or another," replied George, helping her attach the mistletoe to the lintel. "He isn't really boorish by nature, but when he gets fixated on something, boy does he become unbearable! I have no idea why he honed in on us like that, wanting to know everything about us, our plans…"

As he looked up to admire his work, Valeria pulled his face close to hers and presented her lips for a kiss. George took her into his arms and playfully dipped her back like a tango dancer when the phone rang.

"Hold that thought," Valeria said, extricating herself from his embrace. "It's probably someone calling about tomorrow's party."

She walked into the next room, and while George could make out the usual exchange of formal greetings, he couldn't tell what Valeria was saying. He busied himself placing candles in a candelabra. After a while, he was struck that there had been a long period of silence on Valeria's part. She was still on the phone, listening and uttering no more than an occasional "yes," "right," "incredible!" or "how odd."

Several minutes passed this way before George, his curiosity getting the best of him, went into the next room and looked at Valeria inquiringly. With an expression that was a mixture of amusement and bewilderment, she put a hand over the receiver and whispered, "You won't believe this, but it's Ryan, and he's here in Switzerland, nearby."

George shook his head indicating to Valeria that he had no intention of speaking with Ryan. For a while he stood there watching her. He could tell that she was struggling to keep herself from bursting out laughing.

After a while, he withdrew to the living room and continued to put up Christmas decorations, but he was unable to concentrate on the task. His attention was diverted every time he heard Valeria's animated voice responding to something Ryan said to her.

At some point, George was startled by Valeria's uproarious laughter. Then he heard her exclaim in disbelief, "You mean to tell me that you've come to live in Lugano just because we decided to make this house our primary residence?" She stopped for a moment, then continued in exasperation. "Ryan, we explained this to you a thousand times. We weren't trying to hide any complex rationale from you."

George peered into the other room and looked questioningly at his wife. Valeria waved him off and continued to listen intently.

Then she said, "Ryan, Ryan—calm down! All I can tell you is what I've told you all along. The world is ripe for change. But when and how and what it will look like—well, it's just not possible to predict. So relax. How about coming over to our house tomorrow night? We can talk...about other things. We'll keep it all very simple. We've got a few friends coming over, and George will be happy to see you."

She looked meaningfully at George.

"Why not? Even if things had changed, it wouldn't have to wipe out all of our traditions and alter the regular flow of life, as long as a different set of demands didn't arise to make that necessary. So we'll see you here tomorrow night then...right now I've got to go."

She paused to listen for a moment before adding, "Don't give it a second thought. Everything will be fine...around 7:30. You know the way here? Okay, then. Bye."

When Valeria hung up, George came into the room and said, "I'm glad you were the one who picked up the phone."

Valeria looked up at him, clearly puzzled, and said, "Why would he have driven by our house lots of times without ever stopping in to see us? That's odd behavior. Then again, maybe all too clear…"

She filled George in on the conversation: Ryan had decided to follow them to Lugano and copy everything they were doing because he was certain they had secret knowledge about how to survive the catastrophic events that were sure to happen on December 21.

"He's got a house farther inland, on the side of a hill with a little bit of land around it, 'isolated and easy to defend in case of attack'! He even keeps chickens, goats and rabbits in the yard for food and milk, and has someone growing vegetables for him in a greenhouse."

She burst out laughing again. "I asked him if he was expecting a revolution in Switzerland. Needless to say, he was not amused. He kept pressing me to find out if I thought something still might happen, or if it had happened already and he just hadn't heard about it. For the past week, he's been glued to the television."

"Do you think he's gone off the deep end?" George asked.

"I don't know. That's why I invited him. He's been isolated for some time and feels disconnected. Be nice to him. He thinks you're mad at him because he didn't support your retirement whole-heartedly."

The Christmas Eve dinner party was enjoyable and relaxing. George and Valeria had invited three other couples, an Italian doctor and a local attorney with their spouses, and a former American industrialist who, like George, was semi-retired and spent much of his time with his wife supporting various arts and cultural programs. The menu featured a variety of fish dishes and excellent Swiss white wine, which encouraged lively conversation brimming with plans for the immediate future. No one mentioned what had happened over the course of

2012, it having been a year to forget. And wasn't that always the way? Out of superstition, it was best not to extol the past if it had been all too positive, while if things hadn't gone so well, it was best just to ignore it. The future, however, lies open to our imagination—so why not indulge?

Amid the pleasantness of the evening Ryan at first stood out from the other partygoers. He was acting like someone who'd just awoken from a long slumber, or a researcher who had recently returned from a lengthy stint exploring the Amazonian jungles.

When he arrived, George greeted him like a long-lost friend, and Ryan, after a searching look, visibly relaxed. Valeria gave him a friendly hug, although she nearly regretted having done so when Ryan cornered her in the kitchen while she was preparing a tray of hors d'oeuvres.

"I'm glad you were the one who picked up the phone yesterday," he said. "I wanted to talk to you and wouldn't have known how to explain that to George—"

"I don't see any problem with that," Valeria interrupted. "George isn't touchy about that sort of thing, much less the jealous type. You could have just exchanged greetings and then told him you wanted to talk to me."

"You're a woman who knows much more than you want others to think," Ryan countered. "You're profound. You pay special attention to life's nuances and our connections with the inexplicable things that exert such a powerful influence over us."

"You mean to say that you consider me a philosopher," Valeria teased. "Or a soothsayer, a sorceress, or all three. I'd love to believe your flattery, but I'm sorry to have to disappoint you. All I am is someone who happens to be curious."

Ryan ignored her protests. "Look, I need your help. For the past year I've based my whole life on facing this moment, and now I feel like a pen that's run out of ink but still wants to keep writing."

Valeria fixed him with her gaze. "Not tonight, Ryan, you promised. Come on now, buck up! Let's go join the others."

Chastened, he nodded in agreement.

For the rest of the evening, Ryan acceded to her wishes. Not once did he mention December 21—even if he did look rather interested the few times the subject was brought up by others. While in the past he would have insisted on being the center of attention, this time he had little to say.

Valeria had introduced Ryan as a high financier who operated in many different parts of the world, especially in the Far East. She explained how he'd come to town just recently, having moved into a villa overlooking Lugano with the intention of enjoying a little peace and quiet, and "smelling the roses," as the Americans say. Mentioning that he had worked with George for many years on a number of projects satisfied everyone's curiosity and the evening proceeded smoothly.

Talk shifted back and forth from English to Italian, which was the local language, in a seemingly disorganized hodgepodge that served them all well. Everyone was able to understand either language, although some found it difficult to express themselves clearly in one or the other. The ensuing buzz was an interesting concoction that made Ryan happy, and he showed it in the look on his face and the few brief sallies he made.

Whenever one of the guests would comment on the uneventful coming and going of December 21, Valeria would stifle such talk, maintaining that the magic of Christmas Eve should not be spoiled by prattle over the phobias of the world and the hyperboles of the mass media.

When she reminded them that the Christmas *season* was part of a sacred tradition that stretched back to well before the birth of Christ, Ryan's teasing question of how there could have been "Christmas" before "Christ" invited everyone's laughter.

"I said the Christmas season," Valeria retorted good-naturedly. "This time of year has always been dedicated to ceremonies, celebrations and the exchange of gifts in many ancient civilizations. The Romans, around the time of the birth of Christ, called these holidays the Saturnalia, after Saturn, the god of agriculture and harvest time." She added mischievously, "I'll leave it up to you to decide whether Christ chose to be born this time of year for these reasons, or whether the Christians made the two dates coincide in order to appropriate someone else's tradition and facilitate the spread of the teachings of Christ."

Ryan laughed with delight and said, "You love to make fun of us with all your learning and awareness."

Valeria was relieved to hear Ryan enjoying himself again, but she remained uneasy that Ryan had not abandoned his fixation, especially in her regard—he'd simply agreed to a truce on this special occasion with friends.

George had observed Ryan throughout the early part of the evening, too, noting that after their initial greeting, his friend had made no effort to seek him out again. He wondered about Ryan's state of mind, but saw nothing in his behavior to alarm him. After a while, he forgot about these concerns and enjoyed the genial atmosphere of the party, marveling from time to time that he had taken to a life of semi-retirement so quickly and that he had no regrets whatsoever about leaving his business behind.

At home the next day, Ryan thought about Valeria's words and her determination to avoid all talk of December 21. He was more convinced than ever that she actually did know something that others had overlooked, and that she had no intention of sharing her information with anyone but George. He also was perplexed by the strange calmness she and George had exhibited, as if some inner struggle had been resolved and they were at ease with living in expectation of some decisive change ahead. Was this just the natural result of living like retirees? Before, they had been up to their necks in dealing with one problem after another, planning trips, scheduling and attending meetings. Now they actually had time to relax and read and think. Who wouldn't be more at peace?

Yet Ryan couldn't imagine that there wasn't something else going on. In his experience, thinking brought with it doubts, uncertainty and insecurity. And he knew plenty of that—at times, he thought he was going crazy. He missed the days when his battles in the world of high finance kept his mind completely focused on earning as much as he could while exploiting the system. Now when he thought back on those times, he even had momentary second thoughts. Had he been dishonest? Was taking advantage of the weakness of others a good or a bad thing? Back then he never would have posed these questions. But now he began to wonder, and it bothered him.

He tried to dismiss such thoughts as foolish musings, but worried that even having them meant that there was something wrong.

He yearned for something—anything—to happen that would justify all his planning and allow him to unveil his know-how, which now seemed to be wasting away in anticipation of the longed-for conclusion. He felt as if he were in an isolation ward, keeping himself fit with mental exercises that he had no opportunity to put into practice. In expectation of the big event, he had withdrawn from the daily grind of a profession that would have granted him the chance to act and manipulate the system.

Now he was a man apart, watching the evolution of his high-finance homeland from the outside, primed to make his comeback when the world would be forced to adopt a new set of rules.

This wait was mandatory for his future survival. If he returned before the scenario changed, he would self-destruct and miss any chance at exploiting the shift. Yet wasn't that just what other people before him had done, prior to going on to wield great power?

For Ryan, one example that came to mind was Lenin, who lived in exile for many years with no opportunities to put his radical ideas into action. Patience, readiness, focus and a lust for power had sustained him until his moment in history came in the wake of the collapse of the Russian Empire at the end of World War I, when he traveled across Europe and arrived in Moscow, prepared to lead the Bolshevik Revolution. Lenin and his fellow Communists acted with unwavering faith that they were right. The fact that only a few—mostly themselves and their zealous followers—gained any real advantage from their rise did not seem to affect them. Nor did they show the least concern over all those who suffered on account of them, as history would go on to demonstrate so clearly.

As a confirmed capitalist, Ryan did not agree with their discredited theories, but he admired their unswerving determination in pursuit of their goals, and he wished he had but a fraction of their certainty and faith.

After spending the rest of the morning reading the paper, watching TV and checking the Web for the latest developments, growing edgier and more doubtful all the while, he considered calling Valeria for the umpteenth time, hoping to find some chink in her armor and penetrate her cache of secrets somehow.

He was intrigued by her analysis of Christianity. While he felt estranged from all the holiday traditions—practically speaking, religion was something of no real importance to him—he wanted to know more because he was faced with a new idea that Valeria had sewn in his mind.

If significant events that brought about change in the past—the rise of Christianity, for example—took so long to gain a foothold and wipe out or transform customs and culture—such as Roman traditions—then perhaps the events forecast for December 21, 2012 constituted only an initial push. Maybe they would lead to major changes in the current system over a longer period of time. But how much time would they take? And just how would these changes in climate, radiation, laws governing magnetism, and so on, affect life on Earth? Everyone expected sudden catastrophic events of a limited duration, but if these celestial transformations were to influence us to the point of initiating these changes, then what?

Ryan became excited by the possibilities. He realized that he had never before in his life dealt with thoughts and events so profound.

The reason behind all this mental activity was easy enough to explain: It had a decisive influence over his well-being, which meant that these theories were not merely useless mental exercises, but had the potential to become powerful applications and guides for business strategies. He had the sensation he was drawing near to his bailiwick of high finance. And just as in high finance, he needed to find people in the know with whom he could exchange ideas and news to help him make his decisions.

Deep down inside, he felt that Valeria was the key. If he could only reach her and get her to open up to him, then George would fall in line quickly, and from there Ryan would go on to weave his strategy for the new times ahead.

 CHAPTER 13

It was a beautiful morning in late January. The sun was shining brightly, the air was crisp, there was no wind. It seemed that, after months of snow and rain, spring was sending out an early signal to say it was on its way. It was necessary to wait a little more and believe it would come. Basically, this was once again life's recurring message: Hope and believe in a future that somehow will be gratifying.

Just before noon, George decided to take a walk to downtown Lugano and perhaps buy something special for lunch to bring back to share with Valeria.

That morning he had worked intensely to come up with a solution to a technical problem that was holding up progress on the execution of a design project. He kept his hand in the firm by consulting from time to time and sharing his experience with his younger partners. It still intrigued him that changing several parameters and examining the reality of different aspects, and then piecing everything back together would allow conclusions to assume new shapes that slowly materialized.

Knowing how to approach such problems with an open mind and a little creativity led you to discover just how easy the solution was— when up until a minute earlier you could not even spot a trace of it.

That was what his father had taught him early on, and George had suddenly recalled the very moment when Hans had given him that advice. George realized that until recently it had been quite a while since he'd dedicated time to think about the days of his youth. He wondered why and felt a rush of warmth run through his body. He was overcome by a desire to get out into the fresh air that flowed delicately down from the mountains surrounding Lake Lugano.

Now, wrapped in a heavy jacket, a hat pulled over his head, George made his way along the lake with his hands in his pockets, then headed down a side street that would lead him to the porticoes downtown, where there were lots of little specialty food shops.

He breathed in deeply, almost as if to hyperventilate on purpose, wanting to suck in all the air he could to keep alive the flow of warmth that continued to circulate deep within him. He'd experienced it before, but only for a few moments at a time. Now, it seemed to be fueled by a stable, continuous force. He felt happy and wanted it to go on so that he might understand where it came from and share it with Valeria. He was eager for her to experience it, too. It would be a great joy to feel it together with her. Maybe she would find an explanation for it.

When he analyzed it, he realized that the flow came from outside, from something beyond his body, yet it seemed to have some connection to his soul or his world of thoughts and feelings. It was healthy, friendly and comfortable. George knew with certainty that this sensation was something beneficial and not a warning sign of a heart attack or an increase in body temperature to fight off some kind of virus.

He walked on distractedly, ignoring his surroundings. He found himself talking to his father as if he were walking next to him. They got involved in a profound discussion concerning the differences in communication between his father's time and today's world. George's father maintained that when it came down to it, except for the increase in speed, there wasn't such a big difference. Humanity resisted internal change and adapted to whatever means were available in order to pursue the same objectives, good or bad.

They talked of various wars and recent events that demonstrated the truth of that observation.

Finally Hans said, "You see, humans understand their own limits only when their being changes levels, but even then they must deal with new circumstances, which are in a certain sense analogous to their former situations. Thus they progress and slowly transform over time…"

George was startled by these words, which sounded like a statement made by someone who was relating personal knowledge. This was not just a message coming from his imagination, based on memories of his father.

Alarmed, George turned quickly to his right—to the left was the lake—to look for some concrete object that would ground him and banish this fantasy. He saw his father walking leisurely alongside him. Hans was dressed formally as always, only more in keeping with today's fashion.

He smiled impishly and said, "Well, it's about time you woke up! You always were someone given to thinking things out, but this time it looked like you were overdoing it. All this talk without ever turning to look at me…surprise! I hope I'm not bothering you."

Responding to George's dazed expression, he continued. "Don't be upset, I'm not a ghost, and you're not dead. It's just a case of two parallel worlds in which we each live encountering one another. Remember the different levels I was talking about a moment ago?"

George sought to embrace his father with his eyes. His heart beat rapidly, and the flow of warmth intensified. He was not at all afraid; rather, he was thrilled, although he stood there dumbfounded. He didn't know whether he really could hug his father—if he tried, then the whole apparition might disappear.

He realized, however, that the person who stood before him was real, however inexplicable the phenomenon might be. His scientifically trained, creative mind began to feverishly mull over what he knew about the existence of parallel worlds—a topic which he had often explored in lively conversations with Valeria. What he found most striking was that, looking into his father's face, he started to pick up precise details about what Hans was thinking at that moment, and found answers to his own questions without voicing them.

His father seemed to read his mind, too, and said to him, "Don't worry. It's a very real phenomenon, and one that will go on to become increasingly accepted and considered normal by mankind."

George let his gaze sweep toward the buildings in the center of the city and took in the traffic, which buzzed along as always. People were walking about, others were standing on the sidewalk, talking. He wondered whether they, too, could see Hans, or whether it looked like he was talking to himself.

"Relax, George." This time his father's words were even more clearly enunciated than before. "The others can see me, too. Of course, they don't know who I am, but then again, they really don't care. If anyone were to come over to talk to us, he would think nothing unusual is going on and probably wouldn't notice how easy it is to communicate with me and why certain ideas pop into his head. Usually people are so satisfied with their own intuitiveness that they don't realize certain thoughts of theirs might actually be inspired by the observations of others like myself, which are broadcast live, as it were. They can even shake my hand if they want. And you can give me a hug, which you were wondering about a little while ago."

George hesitated at first, and then threw his arms around his father like a child greeting a parent returning from a long trip. He cried out, "You've come back and you're here with me. Can we spend some more time together?"

"Take it easy, George. Don't jump to the wrong conclusions. Are you or are you not an engineer, a man of science who assesses all the possibilities and their consequences with care?"

"Yes, or at least I thought I was, until now…"

"There's nothing different now. All you have to do is find a theory that's comprehensible to both of us, or should I say, to our respective levels."

"Is there any hope of you explaining this to me?"

Hans chuckled and teased, "With every word you utter you seem to confirm having momentarily misplaced your ability for progressively thinking things through. But I'm afraid you've got to find an explanation on your own level. All I can do is provide you with information that can be used within your human sphere."

George pulled away from his father. With a serious look on his face he replied, "Thank you for the wake-up call. I know as well as you do that reason dissipates emotional and intuitive notions. I'm getting the idea that what is happening here is a real event—that this experience can be understood and therefore, can occur again.

"You see," continued George's father, "these kinds of encounters don't happen all the time, although they will become increasingly frequent. In the wake of certain phenomena that will become clearer as the years go by, the various levels of parallel worlds will have many more opportunities to intercept one another. Mankind will be able to transform and evolve the ability to engage in different kinds of relationships. This will pave the way for a melding of the levels so that even if in some distant future the Earth and the solar system were to be destroyed, our true essence, which on the human level is usually called 'soul' or 'spirit' or 'consciousness,' will go on."

"People on Earth are always talking about God, going to heaven or hell, Judgment Day and so on. But the strength that lies within us will take care of all of that by itself, moving among the different levels and experiences."

"I don't know how it's going to happen, and even if I did, any explanation I might give you would not prove satisfying. Each level has its own limits, and your terrestrial level is one of the most limited."

As George started to interrupt, Hans held up his hand. "Enough for now. Go home. We'll talk more about this the next time we meet. Please, let me go. Don't try to follow me!"

George stood there immobile, and tears welled up in his eyes. He watched his father walk away and slowly disappear before his eyes, as if he'd stepped through a thin veil of gauze.

🔯 CHAPTER 14

As George trudged slowly homeward, his mind was a maelstrom of thoughts, images and feelings. With his rational temperament, he tried to digest however much he could of what he had just so intensely experienced, but he kept stumbling over questions—questions to which he had no viable answers. His father had left too quickly. Yet, in retrospect it seemed that Hans had done so purposely, to give him time to come to grips with the whole thing on his own. He had to talk to Valeria. But where would he begin?

When he got home, he called out to Valeria in as steady a voice as he could muster. He tried to conceal his confusion, at least for the moment, with nonchalance.

But as soon as he appeared in the living room doorway, Valeria took one good look at him and said, "By the expression on your face, I'd say you just had a momentous encounter. I guess 2013 is going to provide us with a few surprises. It turns out Ryan was onto something after all. He just got the date wrong."

"Why are you telling me this?" said George. "Either you know something I don't, or you've witnessed something strange as well. I'm trying to make heads or tails of what just happened to me, and I was hoping you could help me reason it out, but you already seem to be clued in. Have you had some kind of peculiar encounter of your own?"

"Yes, but nothing as momentous as yours."

"How do you know that?"

"If I told you I can see it in your eyes, you wouldn't believe me—and you'd be right. After the encounter with your father in—"

George interrupted, "How do you know about that? Were you there? Did you see it?"

"Unfortunately, no. I would have liked to have seen him and talked with him again. But during that meeting, your father taught you to partially communicate your thoughts without having to explain them. I've been expecting this evolution in communication among individuals for some time. I didn't tell you because I figured it would be easier for you to believe it if you experienced it yourself."

George stared at his wife with a bewildered, somewhat embarrassed expression.

"Don't worry," Valeria said quickly. "This seems to be a gradual phenomenon and it doesn't mean that everyone will be able to read your mind at will. In fact, it will take many years and much effort to arrive there. For now, as far as I know, it helps when people intently look at one another."

George searched her eyes. A few seconds later, as if he had brought his thoughts to a conclusion, he replied, "It would be tough, and at times pretty awkward, but come to think of it, it would also make things a lot easier. Of course, there would be an initial period of extreme instability and tension as people adapt to the new system."

"You're right, and I bet you're one of the first to be aware of this, thanks to your strong character and the simplicity and clarity with which you tackle problems. I'm sure that, if you want to, you'll be among the first to grasp what others wish to communicate to you. "

She was silent for a few moments as she looked into his eyes.

"Then it's true!" George exclaimed. "Two days ago you had an encounter with your mother, and you figured the same thing would happen to me..."

Valeria nodded in approval. He had perceived what had happened to her without needing to hear her speak the words that she wished to communicate.

"This is going to revolutionize the world!" he continued with excitement. "If everyone can do this, the consequences will be unimaginable. But...how will the intricate encounter with parallel worlds and communication among different levels work? Just thinking about it gives me the shivers."

"I mean, should I keep talking to you, or should I just try to communicate by telepathy?"

"No, keep talking!" said Valeria. "It's good for us, it's part of human nature—like singing, playing music, and sometimes even screaming. What we've discovered is just an aid. It will be perfected over the centuries to come. And centuries or maybe millennia from now, the boundaries between the parallel worlds will disappear."

"Your father has already told you this. We'll come to sense it more acutely, even if you and I have already put a lot of thought into it. For now, all we have to do is go on with our earthly lives and with all sincerity take part in any possible changes in life and thought processes. Nothing new there, it's already occurred lots of times in this world."

"How silly of me—why am I saying all this? You know it better than I do. There, you see? That's the proof that human beings need to talk, and talk some more, repeat themselves, and rack their brains to say the same things with slightly different nuances again and again."

"Amen," George added.

They laughed and hugged each other like excited children. Their souls, always yearning for new ways to move from one creative thought to another and communicate more fully with each other, seemed to be close to the spirit of the universe.

The atmosphere at dinner that evening was somewhat peculiar. Without owning up to it, they were both testing their new mode of communication. Amid looks of surprise, delight and momentary discomfiture, as well as abundant laughter, it became clear to George and Valeria that this was still at the level of an intriguing game, a process in an embryonic state.

Surely, like everything that exists in the universe, this system was bound to have certain rules for its application and be limited to specific areas of the brain or restricted to certain kinds of information.

Hans had warned that it would take a long time to understand. George felt an enormous longing to meet up with his father again—he had a growing list of questions for him.

Valeria, picking up on that thought, smiled at George and stroked his cheek. "You see," she said, "sometimes this works like a charm, but it's better if we start talking again."

Later, when they sat on the couch together, they indulged in pleasant conversation, relishing each and every word the other said. They spoke of trivial matters, politics, entertainment and their friends. They frequently read the thoughts in each other's minds, but discarded them with quick smiles as if to say, "Now is not the time."

At some point, when Ryan entered their thoughts, however, Valeria's expression clouded. She turned to George and said, "You know, I have never told you what happened with him."

"You mean when you first met him in New York?"

Valeria nodded. "I told you we had a brief relationship, but I never told you any of the details."

George smiled at her. "Are you worried that I will find them out now that we are exploring our new telepathic powers?"

"No," Valeria said. "I'd have to actively remember them for you to pick up on my thoughts."

George smiled at her. "And you don't have to. It doesn't concern us. All that matters is now, and where we are headed."

Valeria squeezed his hand in gratitude.

George squeezed back in acknowledgment and said, "I do wonder how Ryan is taking this new development. It's a far cry from what he imagined would happen. You were a much better prognosticator than he was. I realize now that you had an inkling about this long before any of the rest of us caught on. Why is that?"

Valeria smiled, "I don't know. Female intuition, I suppose. "

She nestled closer to him, and they sat in comfortable silence, letting their thoughts intermingle like colorful threads in a marvelous tapestry.

This serenity came to an abrupt end after breakfast the next day when Valeria was putting dishes away in the kitchen and the telephone rang. George picked up. It was Ryan. In a voice that seemed darker and huskier than usual with an undercurrent of barely contained excitement, he asked to speak to Valeria.

George was not surprised. He knew that moment had been coming, even though he had not been looking forward to it.

"Hey, Ryan, how's it going?," he said unruffled. "Valeria's busy right now. You'll have to give her a minute or two. In the meantime, tell me, where have you disappeared to since Christmas?"

He wanted to give Valeria some time to prepare herself for dealing with Ryan and to discern the reason behind Ryan's strained speech.

Why not see if the new system of communication worked over the telephone? Then he remembered the white lie he'd just told and felt somewhat embarrassed. What if Ryan was clued in as well and realized that he was stalling? But all he heard was Ryan's voice insisting on speaking to Valeria, and in a rather impolite fashion at that. It was obvious that George's calm voice bothered Ryan.

"Hold on a minute, here she is."

He handed Valeria the receiver, but stayed close by to observe what transpired. The conversation took a long time, with Valeria doing most of the listening, her expression veering from mild amusement to concern and even shock. From his chair George watched her with apprehension. On several occasions he was tempted to intervene, but Valeria gestured to him that everything was under control. Then she grew more and more engrossed in the conversation, as if trying to make sense of a puzzle.

When she finally hung up, she let out a long sigh before recounting the conversation to George. He listened intently, allowing his perception of her thoughts to augment what she told him out loud.

Apparently, while Ryan had gotten over his disappointment that nothing significant had happened on December 21, he was still just as convinced as ever that great transformations would take place, having latched onto Valeria's statement that life needs time to implement change. Although he'd resigned himself to waiting, he would remain watchful, looking for the slightest signs of unusual occurrences. As before, he wanted to be among the first to understand and exploit any change to his advantage.

He was reading every article or report he could find on the alignment of the planets in a straight line with the black hole at the center of our galaxy. That cursed black hole had become Ryan's newest obsession. He gave credence to those who claimed that, after December 21, this phenomenon's influence would affect the forces that acted upon the Earth, and that contact would be established with an alternate universe through it. These thoughts worked their way into Ryan's imagination like poison and took over, even though he considered them rational, they were only a sideshow that had been blown out of proportion by crackpot scientists and raving journalists.

But the thing that really set Ryan on edge of late was this: He'd noticed changes in the behavior of some of the people he met—and, oddly enough, even of the animals in his yard. He was hard-pressed to explain it, but it was as if they now distrusted him, despite his smile and his charm, which he had always been able to rely on in difficult situations. That's why he had called Valeria; he was caught up in a feeling of profound distress.

By the end of the call, he'd begged her to come to his house and talk to him. He seemed to be under siege and he wanted Valeria to be a sounding board for him. He was adamant that only she would know how to put his mind at ease.

"His mind seems to be unraveling," Valeria said. "He needs my help."

"When are you going?" George asked concerned. "I'll come with you."

Valeria hesitated and then said, "We agreed on the day after to-morrow. And it's better if I go alone."

CHAPTER 15

The next morning George went to his office and put in a very productive half-day's work. He felt calm and was glad to review with his collaborators the questions they had e-mailed him. They'd worked out a carefully planned agenda in order to save time. George already had a portion of the solutions in mind, but he needed more precise data in order to formulate an opinion, which, along with the others' ideas, would most likely simplify and improve the project.

George had left all the extraordinary experiences of the past few days outside the office doors and immersed himself in the challenges presented. There's nothing more satisfying than belonging to a team of people focused on improving a project and following your advice, especially if you know all along that your job is limited to that function. How pleasant not to have to concern himself with the boring aspects of the job and to leave the routine inconveniences of carrying out the work to the rest of the team.

Sitting at the other end of the table was a young engineer who had been working with George only for about three years. His name was Sergio and although he'd spent a good deal of time at the Lugano office, George had only rarely brought him on-site to projects. Sergio was a man who, after studying a problem, needed, as he himself said, to sleep on it before making a final decision regarding the solution. His proposals were always practical and simple to carry out. George admired him very much and already knew that the next day he would either call or meet with him to clear up a few final details. Sergio was practically the number-two man at the office, working under an old companion of George's named Mario. The office had been run by Mario for many years, but recently the team had based much of its success on Sergio's skills.

The discussion had already been going on for several hours, but time seemed to fly by. George shone brilliantly that morning: He grasped problems in the blink of an eye and interpreted the concerns of others at the table with ease. At a certain point he realized that although they did not fill him in on all the relevant details in question, he knew what they were anyway and could respond and clarify what everyone else had in mind.

His friend Mario exclaimed, "Semi-retirement's doing you a world of good! Instead of being on hiatus and hibernating, your brain's running on nuclear power."

Everyone laughed in agreement, except for Sergio across the table, who stared deeply into George's eyes and said, "My heartiest congratulations. These days the stars are on the side of sincere thinkers."

No one paid much attention to those words, typical of Sergio, which sounded like a somewhat poetic compliment. For a moment, George felt like a castaway adrift in the ocean, who is thrown a rope and is then invited to climb aboard the rescue ship. George smiled and replied, "The stars are there for everyone, and I'll bet that tomorrow morning you'll be calling me up with a few key questions."

There was general assent on the part of the group, and Mario added, "Sergio gets more intense all the time. Well, that's certainly a boon for us. We don't pay him for all the nights he spends thinking."

A few more jokes and laughter followed before they all decided to adjourn the discussion until the next day and digest what they had discovered. When George raised his hand and waved goodbye to everyone, he threw an especially meaningful glance at Sergio, as if to say, "I know that you know," and received a small nod and smile in return.

On his way to the restaurant where George usually ate after he worked at the office—since he had known the owner and the wait staff for years, he felt quite at home there—he called his wife to say hello. It turned out that Valeria was in a store not far from there, so she proposed meeting George for lunch. George was pleased. Her company would allow him to forget, for the time being, the few technical doubts he had brought with him from the meeting.

As soon as they had taken their seats, the owner came over to the table with his familiar smile. He looked at George and after a moment's hesitation, as if he had noticed something—but just in an instant— said, "I'm glad you're opting for the *risotto alla trevigiana*. It's today's special and it's delicious."

Then the two men exchanged somewhat puzzled looks, as George hadn't said a word.

Valeria quickly interceded. "It's true. George has been craving it for two days!"

They all had a good laugh and the situation seemed to return to normal, but on his way to the kitchen the restaurant owner turned back several times. Then he returned somewhat hesitantly to their table and said to Valeria, "And you'd like *bresaola*, if I'm not mistaken, with arugula."

"Yes, please," Valeria said, adding, "That's some intuition! It just goes to show you how long we've been coming to this restaurant."

"Oh yes, I suppose so!" the owner said and sped off.

"You know, George," Valeria went on, "I don't think I've ever ordered that dish here before, but today I saw a *bresaola* hanging in that store nearby and got a hankering for some. I guess we'd better drop the subject of risotto and *bresaola*."

George said, "So, tell me how you spent your morning! Only don't put too much thought into it, and keep your eyes fixed on me as you speak. I have no desire to get the owner of this place anymore mixed up in our thoughts."

They giggled like two naughty children.

Over lunch George told Valeria about Sergio, and she shared similar experiences she had had.

"I wonder how many people are in the know like us, and how many, like our host, can do it but don't know what it means?" George mused.

The rest of their lunch went along smoothly and they left the restaurant having eaten just what they'd wanted. The owner followed them with his gaze, then shook his head in an attempt to comprehend what he thought had actually happened.

"If things continue like this, it's going to be pretty amusing trying to get to the bottom of what we're up against," began George as they headed toward the parking lot where Valeria had left her car.

"You're right about that, although I imagine not everyone is as comfortable with the changes as we are. When we get home I'll fill you in on a couple more of my own experiences. Then I have to go over to Ryan's. I have to admit, I'm curious to see what he's up to, even if that's not exactly fair to him. After all, he's not feeling well."

"Fair or not, he's the one who called you. I'm sure it'll be an enlightening meeting."

By the time they got home it was already 2:30. They saw their cleaning lady leaving the house. She was a stout, middle-aged woman who always looked a little harried, although today she seemed quite relaxed and even waved in their direction. George and Valeria watched her get into the car and drive off.

As Valeria opened the door to go inside, George said, "It's nice to come home, relax and enjoy the afternoon with–"

But he was not able to finish because Valeria exclaimed, "George, look who's here!"

Hans, looking just as he had when George encountered him before, smiled serenely at them.

Valeria, a host of emotions playing over her face, said, "It is so good to see you! I'll leave you two alone. You must have many things to talk about. I know George has a lot of questions for you."

"Don't go away, Valeria," Hans insisted. "I'd like nothing more than to spend the afternoon with both of you, if I may."

As their emotions caught up with them, tears welled up in George's eyes. Valeria, too, was deeply moved, and it took a few moments before they both recovered enough to respond with an enthusiastic, "Yes, of course!"

Taking a seat, Hans said, "You see, I'm more active than other members of my level, which is why my spirit impels me to seek out new ways of doing things and to look for new solutions. All of us at our level are aware of the damage we can cause when our two worlds intersect if we don't act with prudence and choose the right people to contact at the proper times."

"You might be wondering why we have to meet at all. It doesn't depend on our own individual will—it has to do with the evolution of the universe, universal forces, or what we may more simply call 'God.'"

He got up and walked to the window, looked up at the sky and continued. "I'm not talking about religions or complex philosophical subjects, and certainly not the oft-repeated rationalizations by both believers and non-believers, which come in the form of all kinds of scientific explanations and religious dogma. That all belongs to your world—a world yearning for knowledge and discoveries that continuously produce theories and inventions, and convinces itself it has actually created something. Created!

What does it mean to really create? You certainly don't know, and neither do we at our level. But the differences are that we know where creation comes from, and that we are just a tiny fragment of it.

He turned back to George and fixed his gaze on him. "As an engineer, you think that building an atomic bomb, or a big power plant, or even a car is 'creation'? I'd advise you to interpret it as a mere assembling of forces put at your disposal. Just think: You yourselves have been created by a superior being. I'd also advise you to stop thinking that science can show you where, how, when and why creation ever began. Science has only certain elements at its disposal to explain various phenomena and to use them to satisfy human needs, which may be either beneficial or lethal for mankind. There has always been profound disagreement among science, religion, poetry, rationalist thought, philosophy, intuition and so forth. But they're all just different sides of the same coin."

A playful smile flickered at the edges of his lips as he continued, "And since a coin has only two sides, it's hard to figure out why mankind has invented so many."

George and Valeria sat on the couch together watching Hans with rapt attention.

"Practically speaking, there are only two approaches. One represents the observation of various phenomena: our selves, our minds, the world, the atom, the force of gravity, physical laws, and so on. We consider them real as we gradually discover each one. But our statements about their reality are postulates, declarations of faith. In truth, they require no explanation."

"The other allows you, through the application of well-defined theories, to exploit these postulates or declarations of faith and apply them to the world. You can use them to make all the things we take for granted, from clothes to cars to computers—all the things that affect our daily lives—as well as generate the ideas and philosophies that determine our actions and define our behaviors."

"But let me be clear: Neither we nor you on Earth create anything, nor can we explain the origins of all this or the act of creation. The strange thing is that someone who believes in God is said to have faith, yet when someone claims to be an atheist and believes there is no continuation of life beyond this planet, you fail to say that he, too, is following a faith, a credo. There are many postulates we consider true, which is to say, many matters of faith. Why? That I cannot explain."

"But just think, all of these phenomena have their own spheres of action, and when your souls pass from one level to the next, you'll ask yourselves fewer and fewer questions and clear up many of your doubts. You will find that reason will be of less and less use to you as you follow your intuition, the way a poet does when he writes a poem."

"Consider the feeling of helplessness you experience deep inside when you attempt to contemplate the concepts of eternity and infinity. First you wonder why you use those words, which define phenomena that are utterly incomprehensible to you. Whoever put them into your head anyway? My advice would be to stop thinking about them altogether, and you'll avoid tormenting yourself. At your level everything is defined in terms of space and time."

"Imagine, if you can, a dimension in which these two factors do not exist, and eternity and infinity—two concepts so mysterious for you today—will simply cease to be. They will no longer be necessary. If there's no time, then the word "eternity" is meaningless. If there's no space, then infinity cannot exist."

Hans sat back down on a chair and, beaming with joy, said, "Let me look at you. I'm so glad to be here. Now I'd just like to sit quietly for a little while and contemplate your lives."

George and Valeria didn't know what to say or do, but to their surprise they felt at ease and closer to one another than they had ever been. They realized that George's father did not want to be hounded with questions. For him it was a blessing just being there, and the three looked at one another, smiled, and eventually exchanged a few trifling comments—just simple conversation. George and Valeria even managed to tell him about what had happened with Ryan, Sergio, and the restaurant owner.

Then Hans rose from his chair and announced, "I have to be on my way. But I'll be back to see you. Only, don't ask me when—my sense of time, as I told you, is different from yours."

He turned to Valeria and said kindly, "Watch out for Ryan. He doesn't understand any of these things, and I don't know if he ever will in this life. This could be dangerous for him."

Then he hugged both Valeria and George, one after the other, as if that was the normal thing to do.

He smiled at them and said, "The world will be faced with lots of dramatic situations, some of which you've seen arise over the past few years already. Remember, the change comes slowly and never without pain."

Standing in the doorway he added, "We won't always be able to touch one another. For us it's quite a challenge to completely immerse ourselves in your space-time continuum. We have simpler forms of communication, which are no less efficient for those who believe— such as communicating directly with your minds, or appearing in your dreams. But in the past only certain mystics understood that. That's why even Christ had to become physically present in your dimension just to convey a simple message of love and tolerance, which unfortunately was never fully understood."

At this Valeria could not resist and asked impulsively, "Who *was* Christ?"

Hans answered without hesitation, "A fragment of the whole, of what can be called 'God.' A somewhat larger fragment than you and I, but not very different, as he himself said many times when he referred to us all as the children of God."

"Just a fragment, like you, like us," he repeated as he stepped outside and disappeared.

George and Valeria stood there for a while deep in thought, immobile like two statues. They felt as if they had visited another dimension and needed time to reacquaint themselves with their normal, everyday existence.

✿ CHAPTER 16

Because of its remote location, it took Valeria some time to find Ryan's house high in the hills in a secluded area. As she drove up to the estate, she noticed security cameras mounted on the tall stone walls on either side of the wrought-iron gate. She rang the buzzer several times, and a male voice with a foreign accent answered.

"Hello. Is that Signora Valeria?"

When she replied that it was, the voice went on. "I'll be right there to let you in. Signor Ryan told me you'd be coming."

Presently, a young man appeared and opened the gate with an electronic device.

Valeria drove inside, stopped and rolled down the window of her car.

The young man said, "I'm Janic. My wife and I live in the cottage on the grounds, and I do all the work here."

He looked at Valeria in surprise and continued. "You're right to worry about him. He has been somewhat troubled as of late."

Valeria felt a tingle at the base of her neck when she realized that he seemed to have picked up some information from her mind.

"Who are you?" she asked. "I mean, where do you come from? Your accent sounds familiar, but I can't quite place it."

"My wife, Elena, and I were born near Prague. We were able to immigrate to Switzerland three years ago thanks to my background in electrical engineering. My wife works in a bank where she helps out with communications with the Czech Republic. Signor Ryan has given us use of the cottage, which is independent from his house—it even has a different street number. The former owner of this land combined it with the yard surrounding the villa by opening two archways in the wall between the two properties."

Valeria smiled and said, "I'm sure you are of great help to Signor Ryan and he appreciates your presence here."

As she drove her car up to the house, she wondered how Ryan had found Janic and why he trusted him enough to live close by and take care of the property.

Looking around, she had to admit this was a truly delightful place. Perched on high ground, it inspired a sensation of intimacy. Its remote location reflected Ryan's sense of living in times that were like the Middle Ages, when communities were isolated and had to defend themselves, and fortified castles were the best protection against marauding knights and the rabble. It was very beautiful. The only things that seemed out of place were the security cameras everywhere. Valeria could only imagine what other equipment Ryan had installed in anticipation of worldwide chaos.

By the time she had parked by the side of the house and gotten out of her car, Ryan came walking from the front entrance, waving to her.

"Nice fortress you've got here," Valeria said. "How did you manage to find it, tucked away as it is?"

Ryan replied with a forced smile, "What is that supposed to mean? Don't tell me that a keen observer like you expected my home to be any different. This place is perfectly suited to my fears and to my new commitment in life. I aim to survive and operate the way the ancient lords did. All this drivel about humanity, democracy and equality is drowning in a sea of worldwide misery. The world is overpopulated and people are voracious—they want too much. Here's an umbrella term for it all—mass stupidity! The key is to know how to exploit the ebb and flow of tensions, passions, in order to sail these stormy seas and come out on top, which is to say, rich and unscathed by tragedy."

Valeria tried to lighten the mood. "I didn't mean to offend you, Ryan, but you must admit all these security cameras are a bit of overkill. I feel like I'm in a James Bond movie."

"Quit kidding around," Ryan snapped. "You've got to take this situation seriously. You were the one who warned me that the changes that would upend our lives would come about over time, with the passing of each day. Well, I'm following through on your warnings. I can't believe a woman as smart and sensitive as you can treat all this so casually."

Valeria quelled an urge to lash out at him. She probed his mind, sensing fear and anxiety underneath his angry bluster.

She took his hand, gave it a quick squeeze and said, "Why don't we go inside, sit down and you can offer me a drink? Be a good host."

The interior of the house was pleasant and well proportioned, but tables, chairs, trunks and sofas were strewn about the place with no apparent logic. While there are times when disarray may reflect a creative but disorderly lifestyle, there was nothing so redeeming about this confusion, which gave the impression of negligence and carelessness. The whole place emanated a sense of precariousness. Furniture appeared to have been dumped wherever the movers had seen fit to unload it, or left lying there ready to be hauled off to some other location.

"Are you moving?" Valeria asked.

"No, no," replied Ryan with a hint of embarrassment. "It's just that I can't manage to come up with a layout I like. This furniture doesn't seem to go with the house. Although, I have to admit, I really don't give a hoot. I spend my days at the computer and in front of the TV. Everything else around me seems so unstable that I have no desire to dedicate any time to making anything permanent."

"Sometimes Switzerland, with its calm, conventional lifestyle, has this effect on people—especially on ex-Wall Street types like you. The daily grind of that world may have seemed empty, but its pulsating energy and excitement gave you the satisfaction of belonging to some important mechanism—if you don't ask yourself too many questions, that is."

Ryan laughed dismissively. "You don't change, do you! Always criticizing…"

"No, it's the Wall Street world that doesn't change—and you and your house bear witness to that. Big hotels, fancy restaurants, luxurious vacations—all that matters is that there's lavish dining and expensive wine—even if it's all overpriced and not that good. But knowing how to arrange your furniture—and your life—with good taste and in a way that provides you with some sense of meaning…that's a real challenge."

For the first time since Valeria had arrived Ryan looked at her seriously. "I should be upset," he said, "by all these awful things you're saying to me with that innocent look in your eyes—but having you here actually brightens my mood a little."

He paused for a moment, then went on. "Come on, let's get something to drink, then we can have a seat on that couch near the window. You should be aware that I no longer know what it means to be in a good mood. Here, take these glasses, I'll bring a bottle of mineral water."

When they sat down on the couch, Ryan filled their glasses and placed the bottle on a table before them, littered with different objects.

"You see," he continued, "after worrying for more than a year about all those things I told you about, I feel like a curse has been cast over me."

"That's just plain foolishness, Ryan. There's no such thing. You know as well as I do that all too often you yourself are the cause of what ails you. This is a classic symptom of stress and depression…but there is a way out."

"What do you mean, a way out?! Every day I notice things that I'm at a loss to explain. I feel like I'm losing my mind!"

"Could you describe these things for me?"

Peering into the depths of his eyes, Valeria encountered the turmoil in Ryan's mind and began to feel uncomfortable. She recalled the words of George's father, but wasn't sure how to proceed. Perhaps it was best to keep Ryan talking.

"Describe these things for me," she repeated, "and try to be as precise as you can."

As she hesitated, Ryan noticed the light in Valeria's eyes and thought, "She must be in on these peculiar occurrences, or she wouldn't be so curious about what I have to say."

He turned his head toward the window as if to recall the details of what he wanted to tell her. "It all started with the people around me."

"What started?" Valeria pressed.

"I don't know how to put it in just a couple of words, but it's what we discussed before…it seems that everyone's started mistreating me. People used to be so kind to me, and it was easy to communicate with them and even persuade them to follow my advice. Now, all that's changed. Many people—too many—seem to ignore what I have to say. Either that or they challenge me over the slightest things, and the more we argue, the more negative they become toward me. It's almost as if they were reading my mind by the way they reply."

Valeria couldn't help herself. "Of course—"

"What do you mean 'of course'?" snapped Ryan.

"Nothing. Just that it's not unusual for someone who's depressed to feel that everybody's against him."

"Are you sure that's all you meant to say?" Ryan bore in on her. "It seems to me that you wanted to tell me something important. For a second my mind picked up this odd attempt at communication on your part."

He ran his hands through his hair, his shining eyes entreating her.

Valeria had never seen him so vulnerable before. She wasn't sure how to proceed. He seemed so fragile, she felt that if she said the wrong thing, she would push him away.

"Help me," Ryan pleaded. "Tell me what you've been keeping from me."

Valeria considered telling Ryan the truth, but something held her back. She took one of his hands into both of hers and said, "I don't know if I can be of all that much help to you, Ryan, but why don't you give me a detailed account of what's been happening to you—if nothing else, sharing your problems will help lighten your load."

Valeria felt a little guilty, but was certain that she had to play it safe for the time being and avoid anything that would upset him. He really wasn't ready to hear it. Any talk of paranormal experiences in interpersonal relations might frighten him.

With considerable reluctance and embarrassment, Ryan began his story. But as he proceeded he was more and more inspired by Valeria's encouragement to let himself go and give a sincere and detailed account of his recent experiences.

He'd first noticed problems in dealing with the people he saw most often—the cleaning lady, the gardener, the waiter in the restaurant he frequented regularly, his barber, and especially Janic. When he was in their presence, it seemed as though they were all somehow aware of a part of his thoughts. Sometimes they would say what he was about to say, or understood what he was thinking—but had not expressed in words—about them.

Since Ryan's thoughts were often of the prickly and impatient sort or, at any rate, none too kind, they tended to put people off. This problem did not arise with everyone he encountered. Some people continued to treat him as before. Others merely changed their attitude toward him without showing any signs of friction—as if it didn't much matter to them. But a significant number of people became impossible to deal with, and the more Ryan harbored bad thoughts about them, the worse things got.

The problem was beginning to reach critical proportions on the work front. At one time, Ryan used to have little difficulty in getting people to follow his advice, but recently a number of clients and business colleagues had shown active distrust of him. This led him to withdraw behind the computer screen, or at least rely on the telephone as much as possible. However, doing so reduced his efficiency in his work because he could not use his persuasive powers directly.

As Ryan told his tale of woe, Valeria's blood ran cold. She herself had experienced an unpleasant sensation in following his account—all too aware of his negative thoughts. At the same time, she clearly understood what he was going through and felt sorry for him, knowing the test he still had to face when he realized the implications of his observations. Would he be up to the challenge? Even if at present only some people had acquired the power of mental telepathy, the violence of Ryan's thoughts and his determination to take advantage of human weakness now would be apparent to them, which could be dangerous.

"The people who are able to use this new way of communicating," thought Valeria, "are those best suited to perceiving feelings of love, hate, aggression, altruism, egoism, and so on. They're the beginning of this new system of interpersonal communication, and this poor devil will have his malicious character revealed to everyone involved in this great transformation and become a negative example of warning to others."

She felt faint at the thought of such a burdensome task. Suddenly she burst into tears, hugged Ryan and said, "You poor dear."

Ryan drew back bewildered. "What are you saying?'

Valeria could hold herself back no longer. "You're right, Ryan," she said. "I haven't been entirely truthful with you, but not because I don't like you. Just because I didn't know how to tell you in a way you'd accept and understand. The experiences you're having are not just a figment of your imagination. They're real. There are people now who are able to tune into the thoughts of others. That is the big change since December 21, and we're just witnessing the beginning. Their number is sure to grow."

Ryan's face turned ashen. "And you're one of them!" he exclaimed.

He leapt off the sofa and put his hands up to his face, palm outward, as if to ward off an evil spirit.

"I knew it! Get away from me!"

Valeria rose, too, and impulsively took a step toward him. "Ryan, I–"

She stopped mid-sentence. She could sense his barely suppressed rage and instantly knew he wanted to strike her. He was like a cornered animal ready to lash out and it frightened her.

For a moment, Valeria stood there, helpless. Then she gathered herself and said in a calm voice, "I am leaving now, Ryan. I will call you tomorrow."

Valeria backed away slowly until she had put a safe distance between herself and Ryan. Then she turned and rushed out of the house to her car.

Ryan remained as if rooted to the floor. When he heard Valeria drive off, he moved like a sleepwalker to the entrance door and pressed a button on a panel to open the electric gate. Then he burst out crying, sank to the floor, shaking and curled up like an abandoned child.

It may have been the first time in his adult life he had cried like that, and oddly enough it provided a certain relief, however short-lived.

He finally got up and staggered toward his study.

He was overcome by a sense of despair as never before. Everything around him seemed to have lost all value. He was alone after having had such hopes in Valeria's help—Valeria, whom he had always regarded so highly.

He wandered aimlessly about the house. At least for the remainder of this day he did not want to think. When the phone rang he did not pick it up.

When he composed himself enough to listen to the voicemail message, he heard Valeria's voice.

"Ryan? I'm sorry I ran off in such a hurry. It was my fault. I behaved like a fool…"

He drank up her words, but instead of soothing him, they only seemed to shatter his already fragile nerves.

"Ryan," continued Valeria, "whatever you do, don't close yourself up. You need to come to grips with what's going on around you, and there are people who can help you with that. Please don't do anything rash. I'm on my way home. I want to help you. It's just that I have to find the best way—and I know there is a way. I'll call you tomorrow, I promise. Bye."

And she ended the call.

🔯 CHAPTER 17

On her way home in the car, Valeria's mind calmed somewhat. There had been no easy way to let Ryan know what was really going on, of that she was certain. This way, he at least could face what was happening and understand that the perceptions which troubled him were real. Valeria hoped that he wouldn't do anything crazy. Perhaps Janic, who seemed to be attuned to the new changes, could provide a calming presence and help.

She thought of the words George's father had spoken and felt that new insights into the problems of the world filtered into her consciousness, as if someone were continuing to send her messages. How many others would react like Ryan, with fear and anger as they realized what was happening, and resist the new, more open forms of communication? She knew that every profound change in human history has had adherents who welcomed it and detractors who resisted it with all their might. Would this new development lead to violence or greater cooperation?

George was not there when she got home—he had probably gone to the office to distract himself with some engineering issues.

Valeria made herself a cup of tea and was about to sit down in the living room to unwind when George showed up looking worried.

He came straight to her and kissing her on the cheek said, "You've had one awful day—I picked up on your difficulties."

"Yes," she replied, and caught him up on her meeting with Ryan and its upsetting outcome.

"I can't say I'm surprised," said George after Valeria had finished. "This new change runs counter to everything he is about—his view of life, his desire for wealth at any cost and his ways of operating."

"I just hope he'll come through it okay," she said. "I'd really like to help him."

"Me, too. But we can only do so much."

Valeria nodded thoughtfully.

"You know, on my way home," continued George, "I didn't run into my father, but I did have the feeling that he plunked a bunch of advice into my head."

"You too?" said Valeria, surprised.

There was no need to say anything more—each knew what the other was referring to.

By now it was clear in both their minds that a door had opened and that they stood on the threshold of a major change in human relations. They spent the rest of the afternoon sitting together on the sofa exploring the implications, which Valeria had started to consider on her way home.

Based on their reading of history, they knew that the evolution of such situations takes a long time as it passes through various stages of comprehension. It usually starts off with clear and powerful messages among individuals who live in different places, and belong to different cultures. Some better comprehend the messages, others only realize that something must change because the traditional structures are no longer suited to the current way of thinking. Their dissatisfaction often sparks conflict among different religions, political parties and social groups, and destroys common sense values. The question that remains hanging in the air is always the same: How many tragedies, wars and predicaments will we have to face during the coming of the new era?

Since Valeria and George had grown up Catholic, the first thing that came to their minds was the example of Christ and the consequences of his message—of loving one's neighbor and loving one's enemy—on the following 2,000 years of history. His view of human reality was very different from the view commonly held at that time, characterized by "an eye for an eye, a tooth for a tooth" from the Old Testament. Before Christ came along, there were others who had similar perceptions of love and forgiveness, but their ideas had not taken root in the general consciousness.

When George wondered if these individuals had perhaps received messages from parallel worlds, Valeria said, "If so, they called them mystical experiences or revelatory encounters with their gods."

"It must have been difficult for them to see beyond what nature shows us," George mused. "That is to say, survival is guaranteed only to the strongest, to the smartest, or to those who are able to conceal themselves among the masses."

"We are attracted to the beauty of nature—especially in our time, when saving it from human devastation has become a predominant theme. But this idea was born in large cities, where the laws of nature are virtually unknown and ignored until some catastrophe occurs—an earthquake, a hurricane or some other natural disaster that contemporary science and engineering cannot yet provide a secure buffer against."

"Yes," Valeria chimed in, "when Christ was alive, nature was an ominous phenomenon at best and provided a view of survival everyone adhered to: Defend yourself, dominate, kill or be killed, eat or be eaten. In the animal kingdom it is rare to find forms of collaboration. If there is a common theme or law, it is that of your own survival and the survival of your species; order and balance are achieved only thanks to a kind of ongoing war, which regulates the growth of populations and divides up power. In the course of history, this law hasn't changed much, even if nowadays our consciences, at least as far as the Western world is concerned, have gained a new awareness that prizes working with and respecting others."

"Yes," George added excitedly, "there are biologists now who write about selfish genes and try to explain all of human behavior in terms of these natural laws."

"But Christ succeeded where others hadn't," Valeria continued unperturbed. "He spread a simple message of love that is still alive in the world and continues to ply the consciences of many people with plenty of new questions. Christ did not found a new religion, but divulged a new vision of mutual understanding and accord. He referred to mankind as the children of God and considered everyone. He even foretold that we all could become like him. The 'when and where' of it all doesn't matter—for at that level the notions of space and time do not exist."

"Others who came later built a religion upon those words, but it took more than 300 years. During that time, Christ's disciples were persecuted, tortured and killed until the Roman Emperor Constantine made Christianity the state religion. Unfortunately, the new leaders too soon created rules, explanations, dogma, mysteries and interpretations of miracles, all the while covering up the original message. They exhausted great stores of energy and time to prove that their religion was right and that Christ really was the son of God, creating an enormous number of victims among religious, political and scientific factions, to say nothing of people who simply sought to live their lives and work to that end."

"I guess they didn't have the courage to seek out an explanation and ask themselves: Who are we the children of?" said George. "Perhaps many did ask themselves that question, and surely many did come up with an answer—only they must have realized, and rightly so, that the time had not yet come to put it into practice, because the image of God at the time was based on fear."

"Yes," Valeria said, "Christ came to tell the world of a father we all have in common, and while this may be interpreted in a thousand different ways, it does point toward a road to redemption for our material existences. He talked in parables and provided only a vague explanation without going into much detail—perhaps he thought people were not yet ready for that."

"The question is," George interjected, "are we ready for those details even today? Can we aspire to entry into a new era, one that will lead us to another level?"

"Actually, that's the problem right there," Valeria responded. "If we don't come up with an intelligent, peaceful solution—one that's acceptable to everyone and finds a system that regulates the survival of the species and the limiting of their proliferation in the world—then the only valid law is the one we've always known: living in a state of perpetual war in order to control and eliminate others that represent a danger to you and your family, and joining those who form a circle of protection around you as well."

"Aren't you cold and calculating!" interrupted George. "That sounds like a planning engineer talking."

"If nature at our level has been, for whatever reason, limited," Valeria continued unruffled, "who's going to be responsible for launching a process that will allow us to evolve?"

"God? Us?"

"Our ancestors certainly were not up to the task. Will we do better now, if we're all fragments of God, and use this opportunity to understand one another better, communicate on different levels and use what we're being given to create a better world? Or will we waste it, as in the past?"

"Perhaps we should get involved and do our bit to tilt the odds in the favor of success."

"Wonderful, Valeria, you're beginning to sound like Joan of Arc!" George teased to lighten the intensity the discussion had assumed. You know, she heard voices, which may have been messages from other realities."

Seeing Valeria wrinkling her brow, he quickly added, "Of course, I feel it, too; it's what I'm being told. But her story is both heroic and cautionary—she became a martyr, after all. The fact that they burned her at the stake makes it abundantly clear that the world wasn't ready for her. Christ was not alive and shining bright in the minds of those who condemned her. Are we really any better off today?"

Valeria looked at him intently. "Let's make sure we are."

George got up, chuckling, and said, "Okay, but the two of us are just common mortals. It'll be tough to turn us into Apostles."

Valeria responded archly, "Speak for yourself." Then she relented and said more kindly, "Why don't we go for a walk. We can stop somewhere for a bite to eat."

On their way out the door, she said, "I do hope Ryan will end up on the side of light, not the darkness."

"Yes," George chimed in, "he'd be like Paul before he had his conversion on the road to Damascus. He'd make a formidable persecutor with all the wealth, connections and resources he has at his command."

When he saw Valeria's pained expression, he quickly went on. "You really care about him, don't you?"

Valeria nodded and said, "When he and I were together, he changed my outlook on the world. I don't know if he even understood how much, but I am grateful to him for that. I feel like I owe him."

"Plus he brought us together," said George as he squeezed her hand.

 CHAPTER 18

Over the next two days Valeria called Ryan several times, but she only got his voicemail. She grew increasingly concerned. The only thing that kept her from jumping in her car and driving to his house was the thought that if anything had happened to him, Janic would have gotten in touch with her. Still, she couldn't shake the feeling that by confirming to Ryan that his suspicions about changes in the world were true, she had set events in motion that she would not be able to control.

Each time Valeria went over in her mind what had happened at their meeting, she was beleaguered by feelings of doubt. Did she do the right thing in telling Ryan the truth? Would it have been better to keep him in the dark?

In retrospect she realized that she had rushed from the house not just to get away from Ryan's desperate anger, but also to deal with her own mounting concern. Ryan's story was almost undeniable proof that what George's father had explained was happening was truly real, and was proceeding with unexpected acceleration.

Her conversations with George since then had only deepened her apprehension. It was difficult enough for them to grasp what the new changes would signify. She couldn't begin to imagine what it would mean for someone like Ryan, who craved the freedom to do whatever he wanted and was used to getting his way most of the time. There was something of the totalitarian mentality in his makeup that would certainly clash with the aftermath they were facing.

Valeria and George had discussed how, over the course of the past centuries, many old myths had been questioned and had fallen by the wayside, making room for new desires, which had no concrete expressions, however. The old civilizations, based on the divine right of kings, had become intoxicated with Communism, fascism, and later on, the deceptive power of consumerism—but none of them had satisfied the spiritual needs of humanity. Instead, they had exploded in an uncontainable, albeit vague, longing for freedom, without ever coming up with valid answers.

The word "freedom" had always been a protagonist in history's great upheavals. But did the changes that took place satisfy those who had enacted them as they chased after the myth of freedom? Perhaps freedom is not of this Earth, where too many factors and events affect the conditions of life, the flow of life, and it would forever remain a pipe dream. Even today we really do not know how to correctly define freedom, much less find it, enjoy it and maintain it. An almost absurd word—for if we're unable to find freedom, how are we ever going to hold onto it? At times human beings believe they see the road that will lead them there. But they are only deceiving themselves, although it's a beautiful act of self-deception, in that it allows them to enjoy freedom as if they had actually attained it.

Those who live well are the people who know how to take pleasure in their own lives. Not the virtual lives created by computers and special effects, but the ones people based on their own imagination, which ultimately lead them along concrete paths rife with challenges they never thought they would have to face. It is said that as long as there's life, there's hope.

But after that?

For Valeria, hope would go on to become infinite and eternal, and because time and space would no longer matter, hope would be real and could be put into effect at different levels, and eventually reach a point where it was no longer needed—a place inhabited by that which we call "God."

But how could she explain all this to Ryan, a man steeped in materialism? How to communicate such a message in a way he would understand, so he could welcome the new development? Would he be able to accept something so foreign to his makeup, something in the metaphysical realm that he might very well consider mystical voodoo? It hurt her to think that it was perhaps too late for Ryan; he might be too entrenched in a position of absolute refusal.

The thought made her feel lost and desperate for a moment. But then her positive nature reasserted itself and she knew she had to act. She had to try to save him somehow. She was looking for her phone to try to reach him once more when she heard it ring.

It was Ryan.

"Hi, Valeria. Sorry I didn't call sooner, but I had some important financial matters to deal with."

"Are you all right?"

"Of course. Why shouldn't I be?"

He sounded calm and confident, as if nothing unusual had taken place when they had met.

"I'm glad to hear it," Valeria said, but she felt not at all certain.

"Can we meet up tomorrow? I left so abruptly and would like the opportunity to make things right between us. We'll talk and find an answer to your problems. You'll see."

"You think so?" Ryan retorted blandly.

"I don't think it'll be easy for either of us," Valeria responded, "but I have a lot of trust in the future. We'll talk this thing out, I promise."

"I think that would be good, but I can't make it tomorrow," Ryan said. "I have to go to the bank and then see my lawyer. How about coming over on Wednesday, say, late morning? Then afterward, if we both feel like it, we could go out for a bite to eat nearby. Don't worry, though, I don't think our meeting will take very long."

Valeria felt a twinge of concern, like a premonition tugging at the edge of her consciousness. She wished she were sitting face to face with him so she could pick up on what he was really thinking, or at least read his body language. None of his interior musings were accessible over the telephone. Perhaps the new form of communication required close proximity to others. She would have to ask George's father about that, if he paid them another visit.

"Valeria? Are you still there?" said Ryan. "I look forward to seeing you. And remember, if I don't answer when you come to the gate, just ring the bell. Janic or his wife will open up. See that? I like to be pampered and served. I really haven't changed all that much. Okay, then. See you Wednesday at 10:30."

Valeria barely had time to say, "Yes, I'm looking forward to it–" when Ryan interrupted her with a curt, "Good, thanks," and hung up.

Valeria sat back mulling over what had just transpired. Ryan's good cheer seemed artificial to her, but no more so than the unease she always felt with regard to Ryan's temperament. Even worse was the feeling that something unpredictable might involve her in a situation as yet unknown to her.

And that evening it was George who ended up paying the price of her uncertainty. By the time he and Valeria sat down to dinner, her mood had darkened considerably. Driven by emotions that threatened to overwhelm her, she grew extremely tense and manufactured a series of spats with George, claiming that what he said and what she picked up inside his head were at odds.

Things finally reached their boiling point. "You're unbearable tonight!" Valeria shouted. "Why don't you ask your father for some advice on how to behave? It'd do you good! I know he knows what I'm talking about! I'm going to my study!"

After Valeria stormed off, George remained seated at the table for a while. Although taken aback by her vehemence, he thought, "She's probably right. Too bad I don't know how to fly back and forth between parallel worlds yet to find my father."

He wasn't overly concerned, though. Arguments flared up between the two of them now and then, but neither bore any rancor. In addition, with their newfound communication, he had picked up some of Valeria's worries about Ryan, until she had grown increasingly irate and all he could perceive was anger. This was further proof that the new system required time and practice in order to function properly. Anger may not have had any place in it, and in any case, probably didn't help.

The next morning Valeria, after exchanging a few words with the cleaning lady when she arrived at 8:30, greeted George with a big smile and a peck on the cheek. Then she left the house without a word. Around 11 o'clock George called her and asked if she wanted to have lunch with him at their usual restaurant.

"That would be lovely," Valeria said, "but I don't want to go there. The owner has learned too quickly how to read our minds. I'd prefer a little more privacy."

George burst out laughing and said, "Meet me in the square in the center of town. We can decide where to go from there."

He felt better after the call, but he was still worried about Valeria's state of mind. A little more privacy? It sounded like an issue that Ryan would raise, but not his wife who normally loved people and all their various quirks.

"I'm enjoying my semi-retirement, but I should go back to spending a little more time at the office," he thought. "So what if the world's entered a new era and most of the population has grown restless! I'm still an engineer who loves being involved in his work. Without it I feel like my ship is sinking before we even get out of port."

He smiled to himself. Then he called his office and had one of the assistants there e-mail him several graphics and construction plans. For the rest of the morning, he pored over them with delight.

The thing that amazed him was that the kinds of problems he now encountered appeared to be changing. They were more linear, simpler, as if the rules they were subject to had become somewhat more realistic—not much more, but just enough to have attracted his attention. Was the world beginning to come to its senses without realizing it? Was it possible that the rules and the bureaucratic mentality were loosening and making it easier to find solutions that would improve things designed to help mankind?

Lunch with Valeria was pleasant, as was the walk they took along the lake afterwards. But they both seemed strangely distant, avoiding the subject of Valeria's visit to Ryan. The memory of their argument the previous evening had completely faded, yet several times they wound up muddling through discussions—especially when George tried to raise the subject of Ryan and Valeria's upcoming meeting with him—that reached no satisfactory conclusion. The initial excitement of being directly involved in the great changes taking place had yielded to the realization that such an experience would be grueling, rife with stumbling blocks, misunderstandings and problematic situations. Big things were at stake and they could foresee it all absorbing their lives more and more each day.

That night both felt a sense of dejection. They didn't say so outright, but they could read it in each other's eyes: Why us? It was a big enough responsibility to have partial insight into those questions that are deeply rooted within us and hard to comprehend. Imagine the difficulty involved in coming up with the answers to those questions!

Their dampened spirits had not lifted by the next morning. The cloud of Valeria's visit with Ryan continued to hover over their breakfast conversation.

Finally George said, "I've decided that I'll go with you and wait in the car outside the gate."

Valeria promptly replied, "That's funny…*you've* decided!"

"And if I didn't want you to? Why do you want to get mixed up in this? I know you've known Ryan for a long time, too, but he's asked for my help, not yours."

"I realize that," continued George, "and that's why I think it's better if I wait for you in the car. I am worried about you. Just let me stay nearby. It looks as though communication between us and any parallel worlds seems to have broken down. Don't you think it might be Ryan's reality that's wormed its way inside you and disrupted your faith in a new way of life? That it's caused such ire in your soul?"

"Think about it! I myself am pretty mixed up because I'm picking up this heavy negativity from you. It's almost a rebellion against everything we've learned over the past couple of months."

With these words, George took his wife by the arm, drew her toward him and stroked her shoulders, then her face. He kissed her and held her tight. Valeria was moved, and she responded to his touch little by little.

George's efforts broke the ice, and so the morning continued with a different tone. The tension lingered, but the mood was much calmer and there was no more foolish squabbling between the two.

🗿 CHAPTER 19

Valeria walked up to the wrought-iron gate of Ryan's estate alone while George waited in his car, parked around the corner of the stone wall so that he still had a view of the scene. This had been the compromise the two had reached before they left home. They had also agreed that George would not intervene unless he received a call from Valeria or spotted some sign of trouble. Neither of them had the slightest idea of what that might be, but both were apprehensive about what might happen.

Valeria pressed the buzzer to Ryan's house several times, but there was no answer. Instead, Janic appeared at the gate to let her in.

"Ah, Signora Valeria. I will bring you to Signor Ryan. He told me you'd be coming."

He looked around, perplexed. "Excuse me, Signora, but…how did you get here? Where's your car?"

"Oh, don't worry about that," Valeria replied. "My husband brought me. I'll call him when I need to be picked up."

"No need to disturb him," said Janic as he let her inside. "I can give you a ride."

As they started walking toward the house, he continued, "It is strange, though!"

"What is?"

"Signor Ryan told me that today he would be so busy writing out contracts and reports on his computer that he might not hear the bell, and that I should listen for your arrival, and immediately bring you to him. He told me this last night and added that he did not wish to be disturbed until you got here. He said straight out, 'Let me live by myself and leave me in peace.' The odd thing is that he *does* live by himself, and my wife and I rarely disturb him—at least so it seems. I'm afraid he is a very troubled man who's never at peace with himself."

"Why are you telling me this?" asked Valeria.

Janic replied with an expression that was both sincere and expressive. "Because you are a woman who understands what is happening to the world. Your eyes, and even your thoughts, are so clear to me that I can feel them—they're sending me this message. That's why Signor Ryan fears, and at the same time, is attracted by your presence. For a while now, Signor Ryan, without realizing it, has been sending me bizarre messages—filled with fear, mistrust and a profound detachment from the evolving of human life."

Valeria nodded in shared agreement that required no words.

They continued to walk at a leisurely pace because a certain understanding had formed between them. They belonged to those who knew, but even those select few failed to completely grasp what was happening to the world.

Valeria thought, "Poor Ryan. This man's presence must have placed him before increasingly profound doubts," and she recalled Ryan's story about his relationships with the people around him.

Janic smiled and nodded.

When they came to the front door, Janic knocked and rang the bell. There was no answer.

Valeria pushed down on the handle and the door opened without the slightest effort.

"That's odd," said Janic, "Signor Ryan always locks it, and the lock turns several times."

From the threshold they noticed a large yellow envelope on the floor with the words "For Valeria" written on it. Janic picked it up and handed it to Valeria.

With a grave expression, she opened it. Inside there was a letter in Ryan's handwriting.

"Read it," insisted Janic, "it's probably one of the games he likes to play. Don't be upset. Would you like me to read it to you?"

"No, no," Valeria said and perused the note.

It was just a few lines inviting them both inside—Ryan had anticipated that Janic would be with Valeria—and asking them to go to the desk in his study. There they would find a document that laid out his thoughts and the conclusions he had reached. The letter closed by stating that although Ryan was not at home, Valeria could use the house as if it were her own; and that it would be best if she had George join her, so they could discuss what Ryan had written and resolved to do.

Valeria and Janic stood there in silence, somewhat disconcerted, trying to decide how to proceed. They opted to search the entire house to make sure Ryan had really left before going to his desk.

The place was in its usual state of disarray. The bed, however, was made and it looked as though all of Ryan's clothes were in order—at first glance they could not tell whether any of them were missing.

On their way to Ryan's desk Valeria called George to update him on what was going on. She asked Janic to open the gate for him, explaining that George was parked nearby. Then she sat down at the desk, where a small pile of paper lay next to the computer, which had been left on. She moved the mouse and the screen showed the first page of the stacked sheets. By the time she had finished reading the second page, George arrived.

Valeria filled him in on what had happened so far, handed him the printed document and continued to read the rest on screen.

Meanwhile, Janic stood off to the side and followed the goings-on with rapt attention. When George noticed it—because Janic's thoughts intruded on his comprehension—he began handing him the pages he had finished reading.

From time to time the three exchanged bewildered and concerned, but also excited, glances. Without being able to explain why, they felt as if they had been called on to take part in an ineluctable occurrence of great importance.

Ryan's message began with a brief account of his life, in which he made no attempt whatsoever to justify the negative impact of his activities. Instead, he rehashed various experiences without any attempt to conceal his gratification over manipulating and bending the rules in order to obtain the maximum advantages possible, even when they had disastrous consequences for others.

Then, to Valeria and George's great amazement, the chronicle suddenly took a serpentine path that wound its way somewhat awkwardly over considerations regarding his present situation and culminated in predictions for a chaotic future:

...One night there was a thick, damp fog. A cloud had wrapped itself around the hillside, my yard and the house. I went outside to experience this mantle of dampness. It was beautiful—the world had disappeared.

But then I thought, if the world has disappeared, then how could I ever enjoy life again? How could I continue to exploit all that a comfortable life had to offer—delicious food and the delectable tension of sex, not to mention the lust for power that takes advantage of the stupidity of others and the squalid systems devised by mankind? At some point I began to shout, "Get lost, you cloud! Be off! Away! I want to see how the world turns out and how it all ends up!"

Someone listened to my plea—who it was, I haven't the faintest idea. A breeze kicked in and the black sky filled with stars.

I stood still, looking up at them. I didn't know much about stars, even though I recently had begun reading books on astrology and the latest discoveries in astronomy. Those discoveries led me to calculations of various forces that influence the movement of the galaxies and our solar system. My contemplation of concepts like the Big Bang induced me to reconsider several theories linked to the alignment of the Earth with other celestial bodies, the sun and the center of our galaxy and its black hole, which gave credence to theories based on the Mayan calendar for what was to follow December 21, 2012.

However, all this studying and reasoning led to a dead end once the year 2013 came along.

Perhaps astronomy could be studied with a certain dispassion and clarity, since it had no great influence over man's behavior—unless it meant being able to destroy humanity and all that surrounds it in the blink of an eye. It would be a drastic solution that could be implemented only once. Then the game would be over, as nothing new would ever come in our wake, nothing but catastrophes and annihilation. We know that day is imminent, we just don't have an exact date. But what does it matter? In a flash, it would all be finished.

But that didn't happen on December 21. Another force came into play, less clear to us and impossible to calculate mathematically. But perhaps, because of that, it's a truer, more real force— one related to astrology.

At some point I began to feel cold, even though I was warmly dressed, so I decided to go back inside. On the way, I remembered George's old habit of asking the people he worked with what sign they were born under. George, that practical and creative man, had, after so many years of observation, persuaded himself that the signs of the zodiac and the whole astrology trip actually did have some kind of influence on people's abilities and behavior.

Was the Earth, by chance, subject to the same effects? After all, our planet was created by the explosions of stars, and the life force of each one of us seems to have been generated by bombardments of neutrinos, caused by supernovas. We're only the residual matter of entities that have long since disappeared, fragments of stardust.

Valeria, when you read these thoughts, you'll be discovering a new Ryan. You were the one who created him. Your insinuations and half-spoken phrases have ignited in me a longing to learn more. I read, I watched DVDs, I gathered as much information as possible in order to understand where we come from and what lies in store for us in the future.

The result? A disaster, unfortunately.

The confusion that all this generated caused me to lose my grip on the certainties that once governed my actions. I found myself at a loss and bewildered by the mystery of common people having the will to live despite overwhelming troubles.

I understood then why you probed topics related to human history and the future, with vague observations based more on your own intimate sensitivity than on precise explanations.

As for our relationship with the universe and its effect on the Earth, such laws remain unclear to us. Nor have we any better understanding of the transformation our life's vital energy will one day undergo.

I have come to believe that mankind has learned only to ma-nipulate the things and the forces that we have access to, without the slightest hope for any explanation. Thus I turned to the hunches of our ancestors, their simple yet profound observations, and I am now convinced that humanity is changing—changing because astrology compels us to.

I realized that all my unremitting struggles to get rich and use my power for purely selfish gain have turned against me. I feel like the world is changing, but I can't put my finger on how. I feel like others have learned to recognize my aims.

I feel exposed, as if I were walking naked in a room packed with elegantly dressed people—all of whom are looking at me and passing judgment—and I don't know how to defend myself. I feel as though people were readying their weapons for a battle to the death between two separate factions. One faction is trying to learn how to live with the new rules of the world, while the other faction can't manage to adapt and knows already, deep down inside, that it is destined to succumb—only it refuses to accept such a fate.

One thing I have understood with certainty: I belong to the latter faction.

My dear Valeria, I've been thinking this for a while now. And I had confirmation of it during our last meeting. Please, feel no guilt over this, but I saw in your eyes the desperation that you felt for me. They all but howled at me: You're a lost soul!

I repeat, do not feel sadness, but rather, be glad—for you have given me immense help indeed.

By the time you read this message, I will have left my vigil on the big hill that lies to the north of my house. I am going there, following a well-marked path that leads to a small clearing about a 15-minute walk from here, where there's a large, very smooth rock. It's perfect for stargazing. The sky is supposed to be clear and there will be no moon. I will take along a blanket, some food and three bottles of the best wine in my cellar. I plan to spend the night and attempt to arrive at a conclusion in my conversation with the stars. I have been trying to understand them ever since you explained their importance to me.

Lately I have been watching them from my garden and I have come to a realization. I believe I understand what I have to do, and I am almost certain that spending an entire night in that secluded place will give me confirmation of my decision. If this happens, I will continue to follow through on the program that I have already begun putting together before leaving my study, and you will not find me at the house because I will never come back. You will find only these letters you are now reading.

When the sun rises—the star that keeps us alive, and which one day will annihilate us—it owes me a few explanations as well. I shall watch it appear from behind the mountains. Then I will leave it alone to reach its zenith and make its descent to disappear once again—at least for those of us who inhabit this hemisphere. Who knows what it will say to those who live on the other side of the Earth?

I have arrived at this conclusion because I am now a firm believer that there have always existed factors unknown to us which indeed influence the working of the human mind. There may always be exceptions, but all they create are unhappy creatures, for whoever is aware of this flow and opposes it is doomed to feel like a voice screaming in the desert and must languish misunderstood in solitude.

I have become convinced that we—all of humanity—must start over again and seek out simplicity. Only that is not for me. In my life I have taken too much pleasure in using people and laws for my own personal gratification, and I do not wish to change and start from scratch.

On that small clearing on the hillside, with only the sky as a witness, I am pretty sure that I'll confirm my decision to be on my way. Where to, I do not know—because no one has been able to explain to me what lies beyond earthly life.

I know full well that you belong to the other faction—the people of the future. And for some strange reason it seems that you've surrounded me, as if laying siege to me. I know that I was the one who sought you out—but why?

No doubt that will remain a mystery to me as well.

But it no longer matters. I will now embark on my destiny.

Ryan's signature was scrawled at the bottom of the last written page.

If the letter was intended to shock the three of them, it was a stunning success.

⚅ CHAPTER 20

They spent a few minutes conjecturing and exchanging ideas about Ryan's bizarre behavior. They were beset by the sensation that he had either committed some insane act of self destruction, or that the whole thing was nothing but theatrics to put to the test their trust in the future and in some way teach them a lesson. They even thought of calling the police, but anticipated their reaction: "Signor Ryan went for a picnic with three bottles of wine. What do you want from us?"

They were all suddenly overcome by the feeling that they no longer were among those who knew and perceived. Their ability to sense things had disappeared, and they felt lost.

Ryan's letter had a devastating impact on them and shook their faith in the new system of communication among human beings. If he reacted with such disdain, how many others would be like him?

It was George, with his experience in dealing with many crises and setbacks in his career, who said, "Let's go to the place that he mentions in the letter," and they set out in a hurry.

They all scrambled up the path toward the clearing with Janic leading the way.

At first the path crossed more or less flat ground, but then it wound its way fairly steeply upward, lined by trees and small, more open spaces. At a certain point the trail took a wide turn to the right before flattening out as it bent around a large rock. On the other side, the path suddenly opened onto a large clearing on a gradual downward slope that offered a beautiful panorama of the surrounding hills. It was the place Ryan had described.

The reason for the sudden clearing was evident—the terrain had become rocky and extended toward what appeared to be a crest over-looking a gorge that separated this hill from the next.

Their heartbeats quickened. Would they be able to unravel the mystery of Ryan's flight here? Knowing Ryan as they did, they were hard-pressed to identify what kind of demon would have driven him, a man accustomed to comfort and luxury, to spend a night alone on an isolated Swiss hilltop.

They stopped to catch their breath, then took a long look around in silence.

They began their search next to the large rock and continued along the path that stretched around the clearing along the edge of the woods.

Approximately halfway between the rock and the crest, the path took an almost 180-degree turn and began climbing back up the hill diagonally. They stopped there, thinking Ryan would not have gone any further and zigzagged their way between the woods and the edge of the clearing toward the crest. Not far from the ridge they found Ryan's belongings in a small hollow between two trees, placed there in perfectly orderly fashion, almost like a theatrical set. Janic immediately recognized the knapsack, having seen it before in Ryan's house. They also found his blanket, a plastic bag containing the remnants of Ryan's food and drink, and a set of powerful binoculars.

The three continued to search nearby, shouting out Ryan's name. Except for the echoes rebounding from the hills across the gorge, it seemed as though nature could not have cared less about their hectic hunt.

Valeria was the first to voice a proposal, "I'm really worried. I think we should go back and contact the authorities."

George took out his cell phone and looked at the screen. "Hey, I can still pick up a signal from here. We can call for help. The mountain rescue teams are pros, and they have dogs that can follow a scent for miles."

"I don't know," said Janic, "perhaps we're jumping the gun. Ryan has often–"

A deafening noise drowned out the rest of his words as a helicopter appeared from behind the hill and descended in their direction along the edge of the woods. When it reached the clearing, it wavered left and right until the pilot spotted the three of them, then hovered nearby, engulfing them in the gale force winds of its rotors.

Inside the cabin a crewmember gestured for them to listen for a phone call. But the noise was so loud they didn't know what to do.

Suddenly the helicopter veered off out of earshot, circling wide at the same low altitude.

Valeria heard her cell phone ring, and when she answered a firm voice asked, "Is this Signora Valeria Hauser?"

When she replied in the affirmative, the voice on the other end continued, "Lugano police here. We've received information that a serious accident has happened in this area where you are right now. That tip also contained your name and telephone number. "

"What's going on?" Valeria asked in a panicky voice.

"We're not quite sure. We tried to call you, but couldn't reach you by phone until now. We and a number of television stations received some documents written by a well-known international financier, detailing improprieties of many corporations and important figures in the political and business world. He moved recently to Lugano, practically disappearing from the business community. There were also some odd letters. One seems like a threat to humanity. Another seems to be a suicide note."

"Your name is mentioned many times. One letter even asks us to help you in some kind of quest. We advise you to proceed with extreme caution. We've sent some men on foot to meet you."

At that, the police helicopter lifted into the air and began flying in widening concentric circles above the clearing. It descended into the gorge and disappeared for a while, which told them how deep it really was. Then it reappeared at intervals as it made its way between their hill and the one on the other side.

Valeria broke the renewed silence as the helicopter flew further and further away. "Well, if Ryan wanted to attract attention to himself and his fixation over being a victim of the new age, he's done one hell of a job! Maybe his dismal outlook will serve to ignite a spark that will help us to better channel our own energies. He really wants to put me on the spot, and I think I understand why."

George had collapsed against a tree, stepping back from the scene and trying to understand what was going on. For the first time in many days, he clearly heard the voice of his father speaking to him.

"Two thousand years ago they killed a righteous man with the aid of Judas, and a new way of thinking was ushered in. Today a different kind of Judas is committing a different kind of sacrifice of himself, with your help."

"Hans, what are you saying?!" George broke in with a tone of surprise, almost rebellion, in his voice. "What do we have to do with that?"

His father's reply was immediate and firm.

"Don't take it so hard. The role Judas assumed was necessary in order to confirm Christ's act of love. At the time, the Age of Taurus was coming to an end—an era of 'might makes right' in which warriors went to battle and spent their blood in order to prove the truth of their beliefs and claims."

"Two thousand years have passed since then, but that's not all that many, and the warrior creed, even though it has met with considerable disapproval, still plays a key role in governing the world. Today we try to limit the spilling of blood, but if blood must be spilled, it will have to be the blood of those who attempt to keep the new era from evolving."

"Why kill someone who seeks and speaks of love?"

"You are on the brink of this new way of thinking. It will all become clearer in the centuries to come, when people will have to frankly discuss the problems at hand. They'll have to know how to say goodbye to hypocrisy, to twisted and presumptuous religions, to politically correct talk—all of which drive mankind like a colony of ants into a tunnel with no end in sight, convinced that in order to reach the light they must first pass through the uttermost depths of darkness.

"Ryan understood this. In the end, he did succeed in gaining access to the mentality of the new era—thanks also to Valeria and the stars Ryan gazed upon. He realized that with the passing of the centuries, life on Earth would no longer be so easy for people like him, and that anyone who wasn't ready for the changes would experience enormous adversity. The only thing he had was his disproportionate wealth, created by his unrelenting greed, which by now he considered a curse.

"But don't worry, he's doing the right thing in the end. His role is almost finished. You, Valeria, Janic and the others, however, have a great deal of work ahead of you."

"You better get ready for the ride…"

George was about to interject, but the helicopter suddenly came closer again as six uniformed men with three dogs appeared in the clearing and headed toward Valeria, George and Janic.

George looked at Valeria significantly.

She nodded to him and said, "I don't know where your father was, but I was captivated by his words."

After they descended from the hill and were whisked away to the police station, Valeria, George and Janic were questioned at length about Ryan, their relationship with him, and what they had been doing at his home and on that hilltop.

Ryan had sent explosive, incriminating information to the police and various media outlets, some rambling notes, and a communiqué similar to the one he'd written to them, albeit in a less personal, more philosophic vein. The anonymous phone call warning about an accident on the hillside above his home had come from China! The combination of these troubling messages had raised enough concern to send the helicopter.

The only explanation Valeria, George and Janic could come up with was that it was Ryan who had made that call, but they were completely in the dark as to why and what he hoped to accomplish by sending everyone on a wild goose chase.

By the time they finished, a number of local reporters had gathered in front of the Lugano police station. Having monitored the police radio frequencies, they were wondering what all the fuss was about. Fortunately, they did not recognize the trio, allowing them to leave without being bothered.

Once they were home again, Valeria and George realized that their peace and much valued privacy would soon be a thing of the past. Unless Ryan turned up in the next 24 hours and set things straight, the news that a wealthy international financier had vanished from his home under mysterious circumstances while making wild but documented accusations would inevitably focus worldwide media attention on Lugano. Once journalists figured out who the "Valeria" mentioned in Ryan's letters was, they would be hounded by paparazzi and reporters who would make their life miserable.

Aid came from an unexpected source. Sergio, the young engineer at George's Lugano office, known for his fecund intuition, called them. He had seen the limited coverage of Ryan's disappearance, understood their role in it, and promised to come right over.

Upon his arrival, he made a compelling argument that Valeria and George move in with him. He had a large guest suite waiting for them at his house. He would buy a pair of new cell phones for them and install a friend of his in their home to field the calls of reporters and curious visitors.

He reasoned that the respite would give George and Valeria time to consider how to deal with what Ryan had done and to figure out their next moves.

Sergio was so convincing that Valeria and George, feeling over-whelmed in anticipation of the attention they were about to endure, accepted his offer and moved in with him. It gave them the opportunity to prepare for new developments they learned about from television and newspapers, from their contact with friends, the police and lawyers, and most of all, from the voices that now and then spoke to their minds to guide them.

⚜ CHAPTER 21

The question of what Ryan was up to and what had happened to him continued to weigh heavily on George and Valeria's minds. The police summoned them several more times, along with Janic and Elena, to shed light on the situation, but they continued to be as baffled as everyone else.

The names of the people and corporations Ryan had accused of malfeasance were significant. As anticipated, the media interest in Valeria and George soon reached avalanche proportions. At first, they managed to ignored all the inquiries from reporters at their house because Sergio's friend acted as an impenetrable wall. But if they harbored any hopes that they could avoid becoming entangled in the web that Ryan had started to weave with his disappearance, they were mistaken.

Two days later, with inspired calculation, Ryan catapulted himself and them onto the international stage. Another communiqué was sent to media outlets all over the world and subsequently was posted on the Internet. Once again, Ryan explained all his fears regarding the advent of the new era, and his inability and unwillingness to participate in the coming changes. In the spirit of making the story more realistic and touching, he added the letter he had left for Valeria, George and Janic at his house.

But then came a stunning revelation:

I have always been considered rich, but no one really knows the extent of the wealth I control in many parts of the world: real estate and vital industries—mainly in the agricultural, food distribution and raw materials sectors. I have created a trust that owns most of these businesses, which I have put at the disposal of Valeria and George, so that they may use the proceeds to start a foundation to spread the new message that has made the use of this wealth pointless for me.

I leave this fortune in their hands because they understood all along what was happening. Those who are right must win—although, as always, victory brings with it new problems and responsibilities. They are being forewarned—taking on these responsibilities will be a huge burden. They will need large sums of money in order to disseminate the new ideas, help others who wish to join them, and defeat those who do not want change and will actively fight against it—people like me, who realize how much they stand to lose.

To Janic and his wife, Elena, I leave my home in Switzerland along with the capital necessary to maintain it. They helped me, perhaps without realizing it, to better understand the coming change. This gift comes with a caveat, however. They must not sell the villa, or they will forego the use of the money that comes with it. I know that this requirement may be difficult to fulfill, what with all the publicity that will come their way, but that's life.

In order to overcome the squalid monotony of life, most of mankind will continue to seek out more or less valid explanations to satisfy their imaginations and keep their minds active.

They, too, will bear upon their own shoulders this same stressful reality.

The requisite paperwork to ensure the smooth realization of what I have outlined here is with my attorneys who will oversee the proper transfer of funds to initiate the process and make my legacy a reality.

Do not search for me in the hills or in the small gorge not far from where I left my belongings. Do not waste your time. I will not be there, and neither will my body.

I leave you all with the following question: What will happen when mankind can no longer deceive one another and the game of life becomes so simple as to become boring?

Good luck! You'll need it!

Needless to say, these revelations caused yet another sensation.

Because Ryan had operated in the background for most of his financial dealings, the details of his personal life were still relatively unknown, but when news about his immense wealth and how he had come by it were revealed to the public, he became the lead story on newscasts for weeks to come.

The media considered Ryan's exhortations not to look for him a challenge and sent investigative reporters to Lugano in droves. With their creative imaginations and penchant for melodrama, all the news channels engaged in wild speculations and conspiracy theories. Most notably was the one in which Ryan was in flight from the people he had accused and cheated, and the letter was intended to throw them and investigators off his trail and give him time to begin a new life somewhere else.

George and Valeria did their best to avoid the media circus. After they had overcome their initial shock, they met with Ryan's attorneys and learned in detail what their friend had bequeathed to them: full control of his considerable fortune to use as they wished to publicize and facilitate the new developments.

They were quite distressed once they realized that Ryan had not only disappeared for good, but had propelled them into a position of playing a significant role in the future development of humanity.

It took them a few days to fully digest the enormity of the task before them. What most amazed them was realizing how in the dark they had been in regard to Ryan's commitment to telling the world of the possible changes at hand—considering how little he wanted to have to do with them.

How ironic! By announcing his utter hostility toward the coming events, he had made them known throughout the world.

At first, they did not want to take up the challenge. When Ryan's attorney called on them to create the foundation he had envisioned, they refused and insisted they needed more time to make their final decision.

"Why did something like this have to happen to us?" George said plaintively when he and Valeria were alone again.

But his wife refused to indulge his mood. "Because you're a good organizer," she said. "Ryan knew that; he even envied you a little on account of it. Now we have to figure out how to help guide all of the people who have experienced sensations and encounters like ours, and are looking for answers."

"But I'm no messiah. Damn Ryan!" George exclaimed. "And what about my father? He seems to have disappeared. He could have given us some help with this. We need a plan and we need one quick! Otherwise we'll end up drowning in a sea of requests for information and explanations."

"Now that's what I call clear thinking!" Valeria teased. "We'll go work everything out with Ryan's lawyer. You'll take control of the trust fund—we can put his lawyers on that, too. Or better yet, we can get your lawyer friend in the States to help—call him and bring him over here to meet with Ryan's people. We can involve our attorney here in Lugano as well—he's got contacts with big offices in Milan and London. You'll have to think of a way to organize this trust fund so we can quickly set up a PR office to contain the initial impact of the whole campaign. Then we'll see if we can delegate the business side of things to someone else, so we can be of more use to the world."

"What concerns me is finding the right people to work with," replied George. "This mission will require extraordinary people. How do we locate them?"

Valeria looked at him peevishly, "Aren't you forgetting that you've been given the faculty to at least partially read other people's minds? And do you think so many people, including your father, have worked so hard only for you to give up on a task that for some strange reason has been assigned to you?"

At this, George appeared to awake as from a dream. "You're right!" he said with his usual determination. "It's just that…in ancient times news traveled so slowly and people had time to adapt and plan things out. Today everything happens so fast—something passes before your eyes and it's already almost obsolete. Still, you're right. We've got to board this mad train and slow it down, and give people the chance to think and rediscover the joy of dedicating themselves to things that have stability and a future."

"See? You've started reading my mind again!" replied Valeria.

Within a few days George had reacquired all his old managerial efficiency. He tenaciously set about constructing a small organization with a potential for growth. He called on people whose competence he had valued in the past. Others came to him of their own accord, enticed by this grand new challenge. Janic and Elena became part of the team as well.

Soon after, the foundation opened its doors. Like any new enterprise, it required long hours of work on everybody's part, but they were all eager to do it, excited by the prospect of creating a better future for everyone.

Sergio proved invaluable as George's second-in-command. Seemingly tireless, he came up with a spate of ideas and used his ability to be, as it were, on the same wavelength as George, making their work together more effective and moving everything forward at a quick, yet efficient pace.

For a while, all the frenzied activity took the minds of everyone involved in the foundation off Ryan's fate. Although Valeria and George thought of Ryan daily, often more than once, they no longer worried about him, having been reassured by their voices that it would all work out in time.

By now, the police forces of several countries had been involved, however. The Swiss authorities had not given up their search for Ryan's body in the hills outside Lugano, combing the area with expert mountain rescue search teams. Once again everyone involved was questioned, but no one had any more to offer than before.

A number of media commentators pointed accusing fingers at Valeria, George and Janic for having been handed control of such a vast fortune, hinting darkly at conspiracies and scenarios of kidnapping and greed. The police conducted their own investigations as well, although with the utmost discretion—they had no desire to create a scandal without evidence.

The fallout continued unabated. Ryan's attorneys and accountants were interrogated at length. In some countries, Ryan's former accounts and holdings were frozen, pending the outcome of the investigation, to the point that the foundation was, for the moment, left with but a fraction of its assets. It kept operations at bare-bones levels, but fortunately for now that was more than enough to keep things going.

At any rate, the spotlight continued to be aimed at Valeria, George and Janic so long as the question hung in the air: Where was Ryan and what role had they played in his disappearance?

As George well knew, large sums of capital, when acquired by not entirely legitimate means, tend to attract their share of suspicion, and a growing number of enemies of the new era of communication used that fact to try to tarnish their message. Further mistrust was fueled by politicians across the spectrum and, above all, by religious authorities. This was once again glaring evidence that those in power seek to control everything and bury or manipulate ideas until they are deemed innocuous or no longer dangerous to the existence of the power elites.

The ever feared word "cult" began to be used in connection with the foundation, but it didn't stick for long. Too many people in different parts of the world and among all strata of society began to experience firsthand the new system of communication, including numerous people who had initially scoffed at the idea. As belief that the phenomenon was genuine spread, people began to discuss it openly and in earnest.

There were those around the globe who had experiences similar to Valeria and George's meetings with Hans—communication from parallel realities—and they shared what they had learned as well. Encouraged by what they read and heard, others began comparing their own experiences to the ones described in the press. Groups of people came together to discuss and spread the news of their encounters, and make contact with the foundation.

Still, the question of Ryan's disappearance continued to simmer and get in the way of fully realizing the foundation's aims. Valeria and George had almost resigned themselves to being haunted by it for the rest of their days.

⚄ CHAPTER 22

Forty days after his disappearance from his home in Lugano, Ryan once more stirred up the situation in an unexpected way. A letter from him addressed to George and Valeria arrived at the foundation's headquarters. Concurrently, copies of the letter sent by Ryan's attorneys arrived at the appropriate authorities and media outlets all over the world, and before long, appeared all over the Internet.

> *Dear Valeria and George,*
> *I'm sorry for all the problems I've caused you by exponentially accelerating the spread of your theories.*
> *Times have changed in 2,000 years.*
> *As I learned to make and defend my fortune by keeping my computer next to my bed, so you, too, will have to learn to defend yourselves against the negativity of a world that now reacts in real time against your efforts to tell them about the new developments. Perhaps, following the initial push, it will take thousands of years to achieve significant results. Human evolution is still very slow.*

How you will get along, and what will happen in the mean-time is not my problem, but I would love to be able to see how you will manage in this new realm of intuitive communication without camouflage and hypocrisy. No doubt, the new and old modes will have to share the stage for many years to come. Perhaps the people from the parallel worlds have played a dreadful prank on you. I think you'd better learn how to pass through those veils that separate you from them—and quickly, in order to save yourselves.

As for me, I've decided to head for the stars to ask them what they can tell me. Ascending to the heavens may seem like taking extreme measures, but thanks to my riches and the means of travel available today, I'm going for it.

A few years back I procured funding for a certain country's ambitious space program—I won't mention its name, inas-much as it is not one of the world's best-loved nations. It was an arduous task, and at one point I even invested some of my own money in exchange for the chance to be launched into space on one of the test missions. That way, if the world were really going to pieces, I would be able to watch it all from above as the catastrophe unfolded.

Of course, we now know things took a markedly different turn after December 21, 2012. A portion of mankind began ex-periencing strange changes in interpersonal communication. Even I began accessing these phenomena—but I fled from them; I did not want to admit they existed. And I didn't want to become part of a mechanism in which I myself would possess no real ego, no storehouse for all my plans and desires.

If, as you, Valeria, pointed out to me once, I am but a fragment of God, a force I will one day merge with after many experiences and passages, then this reflection comes to me spon-taneously: Either I really am God and I do whatever I want, or I am nothing but a fragment that cannot exist unless it reunites with everything else—at which point I don't count for anything.

A wooden beam helps to support a roof, but a tiny wood chip is of no significance or value.

Valeria, you explained to me that Christ came close to articulating this concept using the words "children of God," which opens itself to many different interpretations, and he went no further.

Telling people they are a part or a fragment of God is tantamount to setting off an explosion full of contradictions, intense discussions and emotions that are extremely difficult for mere mortals to handle. It's laying the foundations for an untenable existence on Earth.

Our being limited creatures, longing to exploit all that is offered to us, would seem to have nothing to do with anything that might be called divine. And nature itself, where survival is based on well executed violence, does not set a good example for us.

One day a person told me that life on this planet is just an illusion, and once we've accepted that, we can be more optimistic.

I do not understand the meaning of such a theory—for one thing, the sun, the planets and the constellations really do influence our moods. And if we actually were fragments of God, then we would be the ones to influence the celestial bodies.

No doubt, these somewhat confused and rudimentary ramblings will bring a smile to your faces—you always seem to dig deeper when it comes to seeking out explanations for the realities of this world.

I myself do not accept this game, and shall disappear skyward on board my rocket—my way of warning the world of impending doom and of the suffering from which I flee. My spaceship will be aimed toward the black hole at the center of our galaxy. Perhaps I'll be lost among the stars. Perhaps I'll make contact with alternate realities that can set things right. And perhaps before I die—if only a fraction of a second before—I may find an explanation for it all.

By the time you read this letter the rocket propelling my ship into outer space will already have blasted off with me on board. The rocket itself will have fallen into the ocean or disintegrated, and I'll be on my way toward what destiny and destination await me. I will go on until my life—let's call it my "terrestrial-stellar" life—reaches its conclusion. Or, if my fate turns out to be different than I imagined, I may live in eternity as a child of God—excuse me, as a fragment of God.

I do not envy you. In the wake of December 21, the world will face a drawn-out period of grave difficulty and misunderstanding, but perhaps that is what is required for mankind to take another step along the path of greater comprehension and consciousness, even if it is but a faint hope.

The following pages contain all the technical data on my rocket launch—so that scientists and authorities may verify its authenticity and put to rest all the idle and foolish speculation that has been going on for the past month. I will have lifted off exactly 40 days after the day you went up the hill to look for me and believed me dead, in order to invoke another ascension that occurred 2,000 years ago.

Not a bad plan, considering it was devised by a man who only operated in the empty world of high finance of the second millennium.

There followed Ryan's notarized signature and the date.

🎭 EPILOGUE

More than a year had passed since Ryan's ascent in his spaceship. George, Valeria, Janic, Elena and some friends were having an intimate dinner party at Ryan's former estate—which Janic and Elena now called home. They decided to hold this event in order to celebrate the progress of the foundation, and in the meantime get some new inspiration about how to best communicate their message to the world. It was very important to them that it would remain only a message—no strings attached, no rules, no religion.

They had chosen that night specifically because there was no moon and the weather center had predicted no clouds in the sky, so they could spend time in the garden and watch the stars like Ryan had. The initial frenetic situation seemed to have quieted down a bit; at least the part that always spread confusion and nonsense was over.

After Ryan's final letter, there had been no further communication from him. The technical data he had mentioned was checked and found to be correct. Other corroborating evidence from the launch—

like photos, film, and documents from NASA—satisfied most people that he had, indeed, traveled into space. But after a few days Ryan's capsule could no longer be tracked.

What a few media-savvy experts had anticipated over the protests of the rest of the pack had come true. Ryan may have been a negative force in his lifetime, but his dramatic and mysterious ascent into space, as well as his endowment of a foundation to help usher in the new era of human communication, made him a cult hero for many throughout the world.

Societies in his name sprung up all over the globe. T-shirts with his face and the statement "I am a fragment of God" printed beneath became all the rage. A number of groups wanted to turn his home in Lugano into a shrine, over the determined opposition of Janic and Elena. A number of his "disciples" even insisted that Ryan had known of a secret portal in space, close to the Earth but invisible, and had disappeared through it into another universe. This theory spawned another set of popular T-shirts that read, "Ryan lives!"

The assembled group that night did not subscribe to any such madcap notions, of course. They were too busy managing the foundation and figuring out how to deal with the evolving new forms of communication and the enormous changes—some anticipated, most unforeseen—that emerged with them.

At a certain point they all walked out into the garden. It was unusually chilly for that time of year, but having some good food and wine plus their heavy jackets helped them enjoy the evening comfortably.

Valeria was deep in her own thoughts, which she shared, unspoken, with George. "I don't know how Ryan figured things out, but in the end he concluded that this new era would have to begin with the sacrifice of someone who personified the age that was drawing to a close—a period that still mixed Christ's message of love with the bloodthirsty aggression of our more primitive natures."

"Yes," George replied in silence, "Ryan convinced himself that he had no other choice than to enact his plan and make it his message to the world. He had been offered a wonderful opportunity to satisfy his own ego, to prove his masterful ability to accumulate money by abusing the rules of the system and in the end committing acts that attested to his superiority over mankind's mediocrity. Like Judas, the betrayer, he made himself the scapegoat for all the negativity of the old order."

"I wonder what he would think about having become a cult hero for so many!" Valeria mused.

"No doubt he'd be delighted," George responded. "To him it would be further proof that people are foolish, incapable of higher consciousness and doomed to extinction."

"And that's why he thought that those he called 'other people' should be his witnesses, in order to spread the news of his apotheosis," Valeria rejoined. "These 'other people' needed to belong to the most highly organized civilizations so that the theory of the new era could be spoon-fed to the masses by the giant media corporations. Christ himself used Roman power and the Roman cross to create a symbol— which remains to this day the world's most recognizable icon."

Suddenly they realized that the stars were there more or less as Ryan had left them, the same for the garden and the house. Could it be that in reality, nothing had really changed?

At a certain moment a wall of fog started to rise from the bottom of the hill, slowly it became more and more dense. Within a few minutes they found themselves in complete darkness and the world disappeared, as did the sky.

George was the first to speak. "Perhaps we are standing in the middle of a black hole that came to visit us. Look for the center of it. If we can find the point of singularity, the place at which—according to all scientific calculations—time and space no longer have any meaning...maybe we will find Ryan. Maybe he is driving this black hole to meet up with us!"

The tension of the moment was broken as everyone smiled and laughed at this notion. Yet as they all turned to go back into the house, each was thinking the same thing: George's comment was a humorous one...but not far from the truth.

The concept of singularity as something that has infinite mass, as it occurred at the Big Bang, was generally accepted among scientists. But was not that concept similar to another theory—that perhaps our individual fragments of life were all aiming toward the same entity in order to be reunited?

George held Valeria's arm to keep her from following the others into the house.

"We should thank Ryan for reuniting us in working together toward a common goal," he whispered.

Valeria leaned in to kiss his cheek and replied, "It is wonderful—trying, but wonderful."

"Speaking of which," George continued, "do you recall this phrase from the introduction of a poetry book that I found in your collection?

> *'You live*
> *Because life of life is born*
> *And no one knows*
> *Where the border of death lies.*
> *Death may border on a new life*
> *And you must live to find out.'*

Valeria remained silent for a few seconds and said, "I remember these words." And then she smiled.

☯ ACKNOWLEDGMENTS

First, I would like to thank Chris Angermann, the very capable and dedicated editor of New Chapter Publisher. In a contest of "who is more stubborn" between the two of us—I think he would win! He patiently convinced me to rearrange some of the text and add new details in order to make the book more reader-friendly.

And thank you to Vanessa Houston, who left a very calm, peaceful job to come work for me almost five years ago. As my assistant she not only proofreads all of my books and gives me her opinion, she also helps with all of my other business ventures. I hope she doesn't regret the decision!

ABOUT THE AUTHOR

Piero Rivolta grew up in Milan, part of a family of automakers, but he left Italy and moved to Sarasota, Florida in 1980 with his wife Rachele, a painter; they have two grown children, Renzo and Marella. Journey Beyond 2012 is Piero's first novel since the publication of his Sarasota trilogy: *Sunset in Sarasota, Alex and the Color of the Wind,* and *The Castaway.* Piero is also author of three poetry/prose collections, *Just One Scent, Going By Sea* and *Nothing Is Without Future,* with each book exploring a particular theme. For more information, visit the author at www.pierorivolta.com.